FRANTOR
SEVEN BRIDES FOR SEVEN ALIEN BROTHERS

HONEY PHILLIPS

Copyright © 2023 by Honey Phillips

All rights reserved. No part of this book may be used or reproduced by any means, graphic, electronic, or mechanical, including photocopying, recording, taping or by any information storage retrieval system without the written permission of the author.

Disclaimer

This book is a work of fiction. Names, characters, places, and incidents are products of the author's imagination or are used fictitiously and are not to be construed as real. Any resemblance to actual events, locales, organizations, or people, living or dead, is entirely coincidental.

Cover Design by Mariah Sinclair
Edited by Lindsay York at LY Publishing Services

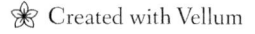

Created with Vellum

CHAPTER 1

Frantor knew he was dreaming, but it made no difference. He couldn't stop himself from walking up the hill. Couldn't stop himself from looking down on what had once been his hometown. Looking down at scorched earth and the burnt skeleton of the one tree that had only caught the edge of the weapons strike. They were all gone—his parents, his sister, the people he had known his entire life.

In reality, he had walked away. He had walked all the way to the first town that was still intact and immediately volunteered for the Alliance military. The Galactic Alliance was one of the two galactic organizations fighting over Vizal. He held no allegiance to either—but the United Federation forces had been the ones who destroyed his home. He had been an engineer, but the Alliance had turned him into a soldier in six weeks, six weeks compressed into one long blur of grief and exhaustion.

But in his dream, he bypassed his training and his initial battles and went straight to the inevitable agonizing incident that had turned him into the monster he was today. He couldn't escape that either.

He woke with sweat covering his body and a tear slipping down his scarred cheek, surrounded by the familiar environs of the converted mill he had turned into his residence. His living area was still dark, but there was a faint glow coming from the thin gaps in the heavy curtains that covered the windows. He rose to his feet, ignoring the spike of pain in his shoulder and the throbbing ache in his lower back and the stiffness of his right knee with the ease of long practice. As usual, he chose one of the windows that looked down the valley and away from the main ranch house, then pushed the curtain aside.

The outside world was completely obscured by a swirling cloud of white. The snow that had been falling since yesterday had escalated into a major storm. Based on his experience from their previous winter on this planet, the storm could last for days, perhaps even weeks. Which meant he would be even more isolated than normal.

Perhaps that is for the best, he thought as he crossed to his small kitchen area to prepare his usual simple meal. He found little pleasure in food, but it was a way to remind himself that he was still a person despite the mechanical parts that had replaced so much of his body.

As he stirred grain into a pot of boiling water, he found himself envisioning the cozy kitchen of the ranch house. Artek, his former commander and the leader of their squad, would be there, no doubt with his second-in-command, Callum, at his side as always. The difference would be that Nelly, Artek's new human bride, would be there as well.

FRANTOR

When Artek had returned from the human town on the far side of the mountain pass with a bride, Frantor's first reaction had been horror. He had enough difficulty showing himself to his brothers in arms—the other males who had fought together under Artek's command. He couldn't stand the thought that a female might see him and be terrified. And yet he'd been unable to tear himself away, watching and listening from outside as Nelly realized how much they needed a female's presence.

She had fled the house in tears, ending up close to his hiding place. He had been poised to run. Instead, he found himself speaking to her. He thought his words had helped. When Artek followed her, she listened. But she hadn't forgotten him, and once she realized that he had no intention of revealing himself, she'd started leaving him small treats—sweet and unexpectedly comforting.

He found himself fascinated, watching from afar as she began to turn the ranch into a home. The ranch had been a sanctuary for all of them—a place they had chosen after the war had ended where they could be together and let hard work and the beauty of their surroundings heal them. Not that he would ever truly heal, but even he had found comfort in the solitude of the mountain valley and the hard work of rebuilding the ranch.

But Nelly had made it more than just a sanctuary—she had made it a home. She had even managed to get Artek to occasionally relax his rigid control. He envied that relationship, and he was not the only one. He had heard enough to know that two of his other brothers, Benjar and Endark, intended to go after their own human brides. It seemed an impossible undertaking to him, but at least both males were young and healthy. Benjar had a charm that might succeed in winning over a female, and although Endark had been moody and aggressive recently, Frantor knew he would devote himself to his female. But there was no hope for him.

Yet he couldn't stay away. He continued to watch from the shadows, feeling more alone than ever, but because he watched he was there when Nelly was attacked by an adyani, one of the few native predators on this planet. He'd defeated the animal, carried her unconscious back to the house, and called for Drakkar.

Drakkar came as he always had, as he always would, even though Frantor knew how hard the other male found it to see him. To Drakkar, Frantor represented his failure. He had saved him, but he had not managed to prevent the level of damage which resulted in his current deformities. Frantor didn't blame him—he knew the other male had done everything possible given their situation and the limited amount of resources, but he knew that Drakkar blamed himself.

He refused to wait until Nelly woke up, but Drakkar found him later and assured him that she was fine and that she was with child.

His first reaction had been joy—that after all the war and death and destruction, they would be blessed with a new life. But then he thought of a child frightened by his very presence, and his joy had turned to despair. Would he even be able to remain on the ranch with a child? And if Benjar and Endark also returned with brides, he would be even more limited in where he could go.

Perhaps I should move on. The thought haunted him. He did not want to leave. His brothers in arms were the only family he had left—the only family he would ever have—but how could he remain, knowing that his mere presence would horrify their brides and terrify their children?

He pushed aside his uneaten bowl of hot grain. Why try and pretend? And yet the space he had chosen for himself—the old mill on the banks of the river that ran through the center of that mountain valley—had come to feel like home. His workshop was below and it had been his expertise that had enabled them to get the power running and the plumbing working. None of the others had those skills.

In a fit of recklessness, he flung open all the window coverings, letting the snow-clouded light flood into the room. *This is my home,* he thought again, and went to the cupboard on the wall to retrieve the one possession he had brought with him from Vizal. A zinar, the stringed instrument that he had grown up playing, just as his father and his father before him had played. The instrument they had used was long gone, lost in the destruction which had overtaken their town, but this one held the same memories. He forced his knees to bend, lowering himself onto the window seat, and ran his fingers across the strings. The clear notes filled the room, and without conscious thought, he began to play "The Lament of the Moon." And then he began to sing.

CHAPTER 2

Florie woke up surrounded by music. A stringed instrument played a mournful tune as a man sang. He had a deep, beautiful voice that filled the air and seemed to reach inside her, making her chest ache and her eyes sting with unshed tears. She didn't recognize the words, but it didn't seem to matter. For several moments, she simply lay there, lost in the beauty of the music, but then reality set in. Where was she?

She was on a mattress in a curtained alcove set to one side of a large room with stone walls. A set of stairs rose to a landing next to the bed, then continued up out of sight. The only light was a dim, white glow seeping down those stairs, but it was enough to reveal that she was in a workroom of some sort. Two huge work tables ran down the center of the room, and the stone walls were lined with cabinets, racks of tools hung neatly over them. At one end of the room, a complicated arrangement of massive wooden gears led to an enormous wheel.

She was quite sure she had never seen this place before in her life. How had she ended up here?

Now that the music had ended, there was no sound from above, and she sat up as quietly as possible as she tried to remember. *The town dance.* She remembered coming home from the town dance, feeling tired, and a little wistful. She'd taken trays of food to the dance, and as usual they had been well received. Although she liked seeing people eating and enjoying her food, it sometimes seemed as if that were all she was—a friendly smile behind a platter of food. Certainly no one had thought to ask her to dance.

As she walked home, alone, through the gently falling snow, she had reminded herself that this was her choice. She had fought hard for her independence, and she wasn't going to lose it now. And it wasn't as if any of the men in town had caught her interest—they were all too similar to the one she'd left behind—but it would have been nice to have been asked.

She was unable to shake the feeling of melancholy as she climbed the steps to her rooms above her restaurant. She remembered looking at her face in the mirror and wondering. Light brown hair, green eyes, and a rather round face—she might not win any beauty pageants, but she wasn't hard on the eyes. On the other hand, in a town where most of the women were married by the age of eighteen, she was considered long past marriageable age. Her girlish figure had become womanly curves a long time ago.

She'd sighed and turned to her books, but then something had happened. Her heart began to thud against her ribs as the memory returned. A huge alien male with deep pink fur prowling towards her. And then nothing.

She couldn't remember anything after that. The alien must have taken her—but where? The only aliens that were anywhere close to the town of Wainwright were the ones residing on the ranch on the other side of the mountain pass. A group of them had purchased the ranch from Josiah Wainwright's estate, but no one knew much about them. Only two of them had ever appeared in town, and one of them was now married to her friend Nelly.

Nelly! If she had been taken by one of the aliens who lived on the ranch, that meant that Nelly must be close by. She just had to figure out how to get to her.

There was still no sound from upstairs so she climbed quietly to her feet. Her cloak was next to her, and she picked it up and wrapped it around her shoulders as she tiptoed towards the door. Hoping that the big wooden door led outside, she carefully turned the handle, wincing when it squeaked, but there was still no sound from upstairs.

As the latch released, the wind caught the door, slamming it against the wall and sending an icy gust of wind and snow into the room. She tried to close it, but the force of the wind was too strong.

"Who's there?" a voice demanded from above. He sounded as if he were standing at the top of the stairs but he remained out of sight.

The deep, rich voice clearly belonged to the singer, and she hesitated, looking out into the storm. As much as she wanted to escape, it would be foolish to rush out into a blizzard with no real idea of where she was or where she was going. Then the wind snatched the door out of her hands again, bending two of her nails backwards, and the spike of pain gave her courage.

"You know who I am," she snapped. "You brought me here."

"I brought you here?"

"I certainly didn't choose to come."

"I am well aware of that."

The same sorrow that had been in his song sounded in his voice, and she felt an unexpected pang of pity.

"Benjar," he muttered. "It must have been."

"What?"

"Not what, who. I believe Benjar is the male who brought you here. I will make sure you are returned. But you can't leave yet," he added quickly. "The storm is too dangerous."

"I'm not an idiot. I can see that for myself."

"I meant no offense. It's just that the door is still open."

"I noticed that too," she said dryly, making another ineffectual attempt to close the door. "But the wind is too strong. I can't close it by myself."

"I see."

There was a brief hesitation, and then she heard footsteps, footsteps with an odd dragging cadence. The light coming from upstairs began to dim, leaving almost total darkness except for the faint grey daylight that managed to make it through the open door.

"Step away from the door," he ordered. "Go to the far wall and stay there."

"I can help—"

"No!" The harsh refusal rang through the room. Then he sighed and spoke in a more moderate tome. "Please. Just move to the far wall."

"All right."

She obeyed, doing her best not to swear when her thigh collided with one of the work tables in the dimness.

"I'm against the wall."

"Stay there. Please."

The stairs creaked, and she found herself peering through the shadows. All she could make out was a massive figure with an odd, shifting outline. It wasn't until he was briefly illuminated by the open door that she realized he was wearing a cloak that covered his entire body, the hood drawn up over his head. He used one hand to close the door, pushing it shut with terrifying ease.

As the door closed, the faint light disappeared, leaving her alone in the darkness with the massive, cloaked figure.

CHAPTER 3

"Now what?" the female asked, her voice low and oddly soothing.

Despite her attempt to seem calm, he could hear how quickly she was breathing and knew she must be frightened, but...

"I cannot leave either," he said stiffly.

As much as he wanted to escape, it never really snowed on Vizal, and even without his injuries, his body was not equipped to handle these conditions.

"Of course not. No one should be out in that storm."

She sounded genuinely appalled, but she also sounded as she had stepped away from the wall, as if she were coming towards him, and panic roared through him.

"Don't move."

"I'm not moving. I'm still over here against the wall. But... is the dark really necessary?"

A bitter laugh threatened to erupt, but he choked it back.

"I… I value my privacy."

"I can see that," she said dryly. "But I didn't ask to be brought here, and it doesn't look like either of us is leaving until the storm passes." A brief hesitation. "And you really don't know why I ended up here?"

Benjar, he thought again. It had to be. It would be just like his impulsive, goodhearted younger brother to decide that Frantor needed a bride as well. He might even have thought it would bring him comfort, but this was more like torture. To have a female here in his home and know that he could never see her, never touch her.

There was a rustle in the darkness, and he realized she was still waiting for a response.

"Several of my brothers went to the town to find brides. I believe that one of them intended you to be my bride."

"Your *what?* I have no intention of marrying anyone."

"Of course not." *Especially not me.* "It was a misunderstanding."

"I don't understand. Why in the world would they think that kidnapping women was the way to find brides? And who else did they take?"

"I do not know who they brought back with them. I was here, like I am always here. But they were simply reenacting an event from your history."

"Kidnapping brides is not a part of human history. Where would they get that idea?"

"It is a tale that Nelly shared with them."

He had not been in the room with them, but he had been outside listening and he had heard it as well.

"I don't for one minute believe that Nelly would have told anyone to go and kidnap a bride. What else did the story say?"

Every word of the story was imprinted in his memory. He had listened and for a brief moment had hoped, before he remembered the realities of his situation.

"A group of soldiers returned from war to find themselves without females. A wise male sent them to a nearby village to claim their mates—their brides—while they were happy and joyous. They carried their brides away, and when the villagers came after them, their brides did not want to leave because they had learned to love their husbands."

She sighed. "I think I know what you're talking about, but it's just a story. It's not actual history, and it certainly wasn't a description of the best way to court a woman. I need to find out who else was taken and make sure that they're safe."

"Of course they are safe." He frowned into the darkness. "None of my brothers would ever harm a female."

"Since they didn't seem to think that kidnapping was harmful, that doesn't reassure me quite as much as it should."

The dry tone was back in her voice, and he had to admit she had a point, but he still believed that they had not intended any harm.

"There is nothing to be done until the storm abates. Once it does I can sh... direct you to the ranch house. I'm sure that Nelly will help you."

He would accompany her of course, but he would remain hidden in the shadows.

"I suppose you're right." She sighed again. "I guess we should start with the introductions. My name is Florie."

"I am Frantor."

"And you're one of Artek's brothers? I've only ever seen him in town with another alien with purple skin."

"That was Callum, another of my brothers. He is also Artek's second-in-command. We were all part of the same unit, but we are not biological brothers. We share the bonds of brotherhood nonetheless."

"I understand that," she said softly. "Now that we've been introduced, can we turn on the lights?"

"No."

He managed to keep himself from shouting this time, but the word still came out louder than he had intended. What was he going to do? He couldn't—wouldn't—let her see his deformities, but neither could he expect her to remain in the darkness…

"I believe it would be best if you were to go upstairs to the living area," he said hesitantly. "You will stay up there, and I will remain down here."

"But this is just a workroom. You can't stay down here."

She actually sounded concerned for him. *Only because she hasn't seen me,* he reminded himself.

"I have everything I need," he said firmly. There was a small sanitary facility under the stairs, and he even had a box of rations stashed in one of his storage cabinets.

"Are you sure that's what you want?"

"I'm sure. Do you remember where the stairs are located?"

"I think I can find them. Hopefully without running into anything else."

"You injured yourself?"

"It's nothing serious. I just banged into the worktable."

She sounded more annoyed than hurt, but he couldn't permit her to harm herself.

"Will you promise to close your eyes and keep them closed? Just for a moment."

"All right. They're closed."

Moving quickly, he turned on one of the small work lights over his desk, then retreated to the far corner of the room, making sure that his cloak was covering him completely.

"Open your eyes and go directly to the stairs. Do not look around."

Once again, she didn't argue. He heard her begin to move, and despite his determination to keep his head down and his face concealed, he couldn't resist a brief glance. Fuck, she was beautiful. Long light brown hair was pulled back from her face to tumble down her back. She obeyed his order and headed directly for the stairs so he couldn't see the color of her eyes, but he could see the lush swell of her breasts and the delicious curve of her ass. A desire he hadn't felt since long before his injury coursed through him. For the first time in years, his shaft stiffened and began to press painfully against his pants.

"I'm upstairs," she called after she disappeared out of sight, and he was immediately overcome with guilt.

He had spied on her, even though she had kept her word and not even glanced in his direction. *I didn't promise not to look,* he told himself, but it didn't remove the feeling of guilt. But perhaps the sight of her would prove to be punishment enough. Now he knew that she was soft and beautiful and desirable.

It doesn't change anything. He could never approach her. His hands shook as he hurried over to turn off the light, plunging the workroom into darkness once more.

CHAPTER 4

lorie sighed as the light behind her snapped off just as she reached the top of the stairs. At least it wasn't as dark as it originally appeared. Once her eyes adjusted, enough light made its way through the cracks in the curtains for her to avoid tripping over anything. Not that there was much to trip over. It was another large room, the same size as the workroom below, but although it was clearly intended as a living space, it contained very little furniture and no indications as to the personality of the owner.

The walls on this floor were also stone, but there was a vaulted ceiling with thick wooden beams overhead and big windows down two sides of the room. All of the windows were covered with heavy curtains, and she frowned at them. Why all the curtains? Why the darkness? It certainly wasn't just for her benefit—she could see everything had been in place long before she arrived. She shook her head. Arrive seemed far too mild a word for being kidnapped and abandoned to the mercy of a stranger.

Still, it could have been worse. For all his size, Frantor seemed more scared of her than she was of him. And although he could have been lying about his part in her kidnapping, he was so obviously uncomfortable that she believed he hadn't been part of it.

Unfortunately, his lack of involvement didn't help the situation. She was still on the ranch, a good half day's journey from town under the best conditions. And as long as she was here, her restaurant would remain closed. She had two assistants, one who helped out in the kitchen and one who waited tables, but neither one of them would think of opening without her. At least she had purchased the building with her divorce settlement and she had some savings tucked away. Being closed for a few days wouldn't be the end of the world.

But then she peeked out one of the windows, being careful not to let in too much light, and her heart sank. A few days might be an optimistic estimate. The blizzard looked even worse than it had seemed when she opened the door below. When the winds dropped for a few minutes, she could see the heavy drifts already covering the ground and the thick coat of snow on the trees. The winter snows always closed the pass over the mountains to town every year, but not until later in the season. She could only hope that one storm would not be enough to cut off the ranch.

Letting a tiny amount of light into the room, she studied the rest of her surroundings. There was a nicely equipped kitchen area along the right wall, including a mechanically powered stove. At least she wouldn't have to worry about bringing in wood. There was no fireplace, but the room itself was a comfortable temperature and she decided it must have mechanical heating as well.

Other than a kitchen table with a single chair, the only furniture was a well-padded chair near one of the windows and a massive wooden bed against the far wall. Next to the bed was an enclosed area containing two huge millstones. The massive wooden gears downstairs suddenly made sense. This must once have been intended as a mill, although everything looked untouched. Had it ever been put into production?

In addition to founding the town of Wainwright, Josiah Wainwright had built the ranch as a home for his bride. According to the town legends, his bride had never arrived. He had become more and more of a recluse as the years passed, although he continued to employ a small staff to keep the ranch running until near to the end.

The ranch had always struck her as a sad and lonely place. The thought of Frantor alone in the darkness only added to that impression. *But it's changing*, she reminded herself. Frantor and his brothers were here now, and a bride had finally come to the ranch when Nelly married her alien.

She sighed and returned to her explorations. There were two doors in the wall next to the kitchen. The first opened into a well-equipped pantry, the shelves stocked with glass jars filled with an astonishing variety of preserved fruits and vegetables. More supplies filled the lower cabinets, and there was a cold storage unit on the outside wall stocked with meat.

She opened the second door and gasped. It was a bathroom, but unlike any bathroom she had seen before. Although Josiah's emphasis on the advantages of the past hadn't gone as far as prohibiting modern plumbing, most of the bathrooms in Wainwright were no more than utilitarian. This was anything but.

The floor was made of the same stone as the walls, but it had been worked into big smooth slabs. A wooden partition separated the toilet area from the rest of the room, and there was a long counter with a big sink, also carved from stone. No mirror above the sink, she noticed, but she was far more interested in the tub that completely filled the far end of the room. Also made from stone, it was raised in front of a giant window that overlooked the river below and the mountains on the other side of the valley. The tub was already filled with gently steaming water, with an area in front of it for washing before entering. She gave it a longing glance, but although she wasn't afraid of Frantor, she wasn't quite ready to be naked in the same building as a strange male.

As she wandered aimlessly back into the main room, her stomach growled, and she gave the kitchen a considering look. She thought for a moment, then crossed to the head of the stairs.

"Frantor?" she called.

"Don't come down," he said immediately, an unmistakable note of anxiety in that deep, beautiful voice.

"I'm not. I was just thinking of cooking some breakfast. Would that be all right with you?"

"Of course. You may help yourself to anything you wish."

"Thank you." She bit her lip, then hurried on. "Would it be all right if I opened one of the curtains? It would really be much easier to cook if I could see what I was doing. I promise I'll stay up here."

He was silent for so long that she was afraid he was going to deny her request.

"All right," he said finally. "If you promise."

"I do," she said quickly and hurried over to the windows before he changed his mind.

She opened the curtains on the window next to the kitchen and shook her head at the heavily falling snow before returning to the pantry to inspect the supplies more closely. There was a pot of unflavored grain on the stove that would serve as a base for the meal, and she set to work, humming as she concentrated on the familiar tasks. She loved cooking, she always had. It was the one interest she had shared with the aunt who raised her, and all her happiest memories seem to revolve around a kitchen.

As soon as the food was ready, she started to dish it out, then hesitated, looking at the small table. She was absolutely certain that he would not join her. She covered the plates and returned to the stairs.

"I made breakfast."

"Good. I hope you found everything you wanted."

"Yes, you're very well supplied. At least we don't have to worry about starving to death. But how do you want to get your food? I don't think I can walk down the stairs with my eyes closed."

She could almost feel his astonishment in the silence that followed.

"You cooked for me?" he asked slowly.

"Of course I did. It's your food, and you're being nice enough to share it with me."

"You didn't need to do that."

"I wanted to do it. Anyway, it's just as easy to cook for two as it is to cook for one. But now I don't know how to bring it to you. Unless you want to come and join me?"

"No."

She had expected the refusal, but she was still disappointed.

"How about this? I'll bring your plate halfway down and leave it on the landing. Then I'll come back up here and move over to the other side of the room while you get it."

"That would be… acceptable," he said at last.

"Good. Then that's the plan. I'll be right back." She hurried over to pick up his plate and then started down the stairs. "I'm coming down, but I'm not looking."

Even though she really, really wanted to look. But she'd made a promise, so she carried the plate down, set it on the steps with a mug of tea, then returned upstairs, keeping her eyes firmly on the wall as she crossed over to the big bed.

She heard the stairs creak, but deliberately kept her head turned away, despite the temptation to peek. Once he told her that it was clear, she returned to the kitchen for her own plate, then looked at the table and sighed. Meals were much better when they were shared. She carried her own plate over to the stairs.

"If you don't mind, I'm going to sit here on the top step. I promise I won't come down," she added quickly.

"I don't understand."

She shrugged, even though she knew he couldn't see her. "I prefer sharing my meals, and I figured this was as close as you would let me get. We could even talk a little, if you want to."

"I have nothing to say," he said stiffly, and she sighed, already regretting her decision. "But I would like to know more about you," he continued.

"Me? I'm not very interesting. I moved to Wainwright about five years ago, and I run the diner in town."

"You are an excellent cook. I'm sure it must be a success."

"It's not a fancy place but it's what I wanted—a place where people can feel comfortable and enjoy a good meal."

"Are you from Wainwright?"

"No. I moved here after my divorce."

A fact she had been very careful to keep concealed from the citizens of Wainwright. Josiah had laid down a very strict set of social guidelines based on Earth's distant past, and divorce was certainly not acceptable.

"Divorce? I do not have a translation for this word."

"It means we are no longer married. Mated, as you put it."

"But a mate bond is for life."

He sounded horrified at the idea, and she scowled down into the darkness below.

"Not in this case. Thank goodness."

"You were... unhappy?"

"Extremely. My husband was a doctor. He didn't want a real wife—an actual partner. He only wanted someone to run his office and clean his house and cook his meals. And warm his bed on the odd occasions he decided he needed a physical release."

She knew she sounded bitter, but it still stung, even after all these years. She had married him with such high hopes—romantic, impractical hopes—only to find out that he had absolutely no romantic interest in her at all.

"Perhaps this divorce is a good thing. A foolish male like that does not deserve a female such as you."

Her annoyance vanished at the sincerity in his voice.

"I certainly think so." No matter how hard it had been to make the break.

He asked her more about her life in Wainwright, but he revealed absolutely nothing about his own life. Still, she found herself regretting it when the meal came to an end. Hopefully it would just take time for him to open up to her. She cast a rueful glance at the window, currently veiled in white. It looked as though he was going to have plenty of time.

CHAPTER 5

Frantor listened in fascination as Florie talked about her past. She had a self-deprecating sense of humor and a cheerful optimism despite what he was sure had been a difficult life. How could any male have been so foolish as to let her go? He would never have made such a mistake. But then he would never be lucky enough to have a female of his own.

Despite that, he found himself creeping closer and closer until he was standing in the shadows at the bottom of the stairs. He couldn't see her, only the faint shadows of her gestures, her hands moving as she talked, but it felt as if they were close. He could even catch the faint elusive sweetness that seemed to linger about her, and he found himself trying to identify it. It wasn't floral, but...

"You smell like cookies," he burst out as he finally recognized it. The sweet treats were a human invention that Nelly had brought to the ranch, and she had insisted on leaving them out for him.

He was immediately horrified at his outburst, but she only laughed.

"That doesn't really surprise me. I do a lot of baking. But I didn't expect you to be familiar with cookies."

"Nelly makes them for my brothers. And me."

There was a moment of silence.

"You mean that Nelly has seen you?"

Why did she sound as if that distressed her? It would be far more distressing if Nelly had actually seen him.

"No," he said quickly. "But she leaves them for me."

She made a noncommittal sound, and then he heard her rise to her feet. He immediately drew even further back into the shadows, although he didn't believe that she would break her promise and come downstairs.

"I'm going to clean up now. Can you leave your plate on the stairs when you're through?"

"I have finished. It was… delicious."

So delicious that he had inhaled every mouthful, barely able to prevent himself from groaning.

"It wasn't anything fancy, but I'm glad you enjoyed it."

"I never learned to cook. None of us did."

In his case, he had spent his student years frequenting the noodle stalls that were so common in his university town. After he began work, he was so busy that it was easier just to pick up a quick meal on his way home.

"Nelly has been cooking for my brothers," he added, unable to completely suppress the pang of envy.

Based on their blissful expressions and the way they rhapsodized about her meals, she was an excellent cook.

"You mean to say that Artek married her and brought her here just to cook for all of you?"

Her tone was clearly indignant, and he hurried to reassure her.

"That was not why he married her," he said quickly. "She does cook for the others, but she makes them work for their meals."

He couldn't entirely suppress his amusement at the way all of them had hurried to perform their chores in exchange for her cooking. His voice must have reflected his amusement because she laughed.

"Now that sounds more like Nelly." She hesitated. "But are you sure that isn't why Artek married her?"

"I'm sure, although she also thought so at first. I... talked to her and suggested that she at least give him a chance to explain."

"So she has seen you."

"I told you that she has not. I was... concealed outside the ranch house, and I remained that way while we spoke."

He had been drawn there by curiosity and dread—and envy. He had no intention of revealing himself and when Nelly had run crying from the house, his first reaction was to flee. But she was so obviously distressed that he found himself wanting to comfort her instead. No matter his own conflicted feelings about the presence of a female in the valley, he had seen enough of the way that Artek looked at her to know this was far more than a practical arrangement.

"Do you always remain in the shadows?" she asked softly.

"Not always, but I am most comfortable here." There was an expectant silence even though she didn't ask the obvious question. "I am... deformed. Because of the war."

"That's no reason to—"

"Enough," he growled, loud enough that even he winced. "It is not a topic for discussion. Thank you for the meal, but you do not need to cook for me again."

He strode to the far corner of the workroom, leaning against the cold stone as his good hand clenched reflexively. He could not allow this. Could not allow that hint of sympathy and promise of understanding to lure him into revealing himself. In that terrible, confused time after the war ended and before they made their way to the solitude at the ranch, he'd seen the way people reacted to him. He couldn't stand the thought of that same look of horror on her face.

But even in the far corner of the workroom, he could still hear her.

"Put your plate on the stairs whenever you're ready."

She didn't even sound upset by his outburst. It wasn't long before he found himself drawn out of his corner, listening to her move around upstairs and trying to envision what she was doing. He would have distracted himself by work, but the small amount of light coming from upstairs wasn't enough for him to work. If he turned on one of his work lights, he would be visible if she decided to come downstairs. He wanted to believe that she would keep her word, but it was only natural that she would be curious. He didn't have the courage to take the chance. Instead, he paced back and forth until he realized that he was following the same path that she was following overhead. As if they were dancing together despite the separation between them.

Fuck. Now that the idea had come to him, he couldn't escape it. He had enjoyed dancing once. What would it be like to hold her in his arms, to have her soft body brushing against his as they whirled and swayed in time to the music?

Once again, his cock began to stiffen—a frustrating, infuriating reminder of the fact that he was still a male. That part of him was still intact. Perhaps it would have been better if it was not.

He tried to force himself to ignore his newly awakened body, but after all these sterile years, his cock was suddenly as eager as that of an untried male.

Delicious smells began to waft down from above and he found himself regretting telling her not to feed him. *It's for the best*, he told himself. The last thing he needed right now were any more reminders of the male he had once been. That didn't stop him from standing at the bottom of the stairs, breathing in the delicious fragrance, and he was standing there when he heard her approach.

"I'm bringing your plate down."

"I told you not to cook for me."

"And I told you that it was just as easy to cook for two as it was for one. I'm bringing this down whether you like it or not, so do whatever you need to do."

There was no reproof in her voice, and somehow that gave him the courage to remain in the shadows at the base of the stairs as she walked down to the landing. She made no attempt to look down into the workroom, but he caught a glimpse of her. His mouth went dry and his cock pounded as she bent over to place a covered dish on the stair landing, the fabric of her skirt clinging to that deliciously round, full ass. So much blood rushed to his cock that he actually felt dizzy, and he had to clench his fist on the stair post to maintain his balance as she disappeared back upstairs.

"Let me know when you're ready for me to pick it up. And if you'd like company while you eat," she added softly before she moved away.

He knew it was a bad idea. He knew that giving into temptation now would only make his loneliness so much worse in the long run. Despite that, he knew that he would retrieve the food she had prepared for him, and he knew he would ask her to sit on the stairs and talk to him. For a few precious moments, he would be as close to normal as it was possible for him to be.

CHAPTER 6

Florie paced restlessly over to the window and back again. She was used to working; she was not used to this enforced idleness. Dinner was in the oven, and she had a tray of cookies ready to go in once she took it out. She'd had to improvise based on the ingredients that Frantor had in his pantry, but she hoped they turned out as well as Nelly's cookies. It was silly to feel competitive with her friend, but he had seemed so obviously entranced by the idea. Or was he entranced by Nelly?

She had wondered at first, especially since he had apparently spoken to her quite willingly, but she eventually decided that he was more pleased by the fact that his former commander had found a bride. She hadn't been sure if he would ask her to join him, but he had, and she had taken her previous position at the top of the stairs while they ate the midday meal.

He had actually opened up a little, still not about himself, but about the other males who shared the ranch. His affection for all of them was quite clear, as well as his deep respect for Artek.

He had even revealed that one of them, Drakkar, was the medic who had cared for him when he was injured. She suspected he'd regretted saying even that much because he'd quickly changed the subject.

Were his injuries that terrible, she wondered as she stared at the blinding whiteness outside. Most of Mathew's cases had been simple enough—common ailments and household injuries—but a few had been more challenging. He never liked those and usually did his best to refer them to someone else, but she remembered one in particular. Oreg, a grizzled old man who had lost a leg and suffered radiation burns during an incident on a spaceship. Despite that, he'd retained his sense of humor, stepping into the office with a twinkle in his eyes and an obscene joke on his lips. But then he'd always had someone with him—his wife Ruthie, a birdlike old woman who shook her head at her husband's antics but clearly adored him.

Had there ever been anyone for Frantor? His brothers perhaps, but had they known how to reach him?

"And why am I even worried about it?" she muttered to herself.

She couldn't fix him, especially if he did not want to be fixed. This was just a brief interlude, and as soon as the snow cleared, she would be heading back to her restaurant and the life she'd made for herself. But despite that, her thoughts kept returning to the big, solitary figure in the workroom below. She sighed and made another circuit around the room.

This time, she paused at the sight of the instrument lying on his chair. No doubt it was the one he'd been playing when she woke, and she picked it up carefully. It had a diamond-shaped body and two long, thin necks. She ran her thumb across the strings, the resulting note louder than she had intended, and she jumped guiltily.

"I'm sorry," she called down the stairs. "I was just curious about the instrument."

"It's called a zinar."

His voice was surprisingly close, as if he were standing at the bottom of the stairs, and once again she was tempted to peek. Was he really as large as she remembered, or had that been her imagination? And why did she find that thought so appealing? She was not a small woman, but that brief encounter had left her feeling almost dainty by comparison.

"Do you play?"

She shook her head before remembering that he couldn't see her.

"My aunt raised me, and she did not approve of such foolish endeavors."

Aunt Martha had been an eminently practical woman who insisted that Florie concentrate on her education and on learning how to run a household—not necessarily in that order. For a determined spinster, she had been surprisingly satisfied by Florie's marriage to Mathew. Maybe it was just as well that she hadn't lived to see it fall apart.

"Perhaps you could learn," he suggested, and she gave the instrument a doubtful look.

"I'm not even sure where to begin."

"Curl your fingers around the upper neck so you can press your fingertips against the strings. Hold down the first two strings, then use your thumb to strum across all of them."

It sounded easy enough, but the result was a discordant note that made her wince.

"It takes time," he said, his deep voice calm. "Try again with a little more pressure on the strings."

Her second attempt was no more successful than the first, but he did his best to try and instruct her until she finally sighed and gave up.

"I just don't seem to be getting it. I wish you could just show me."

She immediately felt the tension emanating from the darkness below.

"That is not going to happen."

His voice had turned stiff once again, but she was sure that there was a hint of longing in it as well, and that gave her the courage to push a little harder.

"What if I closed all the curtains? You could keep your cloak on. All I need to see is your hands."

He didn't respond immediately, and she hoped he was considering it. She really wanted to see him again, even hidden in his cloak. She wanted him to be more than just a disembodied voice from below.

"No," he said finally, and she sighed.

"All right. But I hope you'll change your mind. I'm not going to judge you."

He didn't respond, and she sighed again and went to attend to dinner.

Once again she sat at the top of the stairs as they ate but they talked little. The periods of silence weren't uncomfortable, but he seemed distracted and she found herself equally thoughtful. The past few years had been so busy that she'd had little time to think of the past. This evening, she found herself thinking about her aunt. Their relationship had been strained at times, but once she was out on her own, she began to suspect that her aunt's insistence on practical matters had been out of concern for her. Aunt Martha had given her the tools she needed to make her own way in the world, and perhaps that was what she had intended all along. She wished they'd had more time together.

Determined to shake off the unexpected melancholy, she jumped up and went to retrieve the cookies.

"I'm coming down again. Just as far as the landing," she added quickly.

"Why?"

"It's a surprise."

She hurried down to put the plate of cookies on the landing. As she turned to come back upstairs, she was sure she caught a glimpse of movement in the darkness, but she forced herself not to linger.

"What is that?" he asked.

"Find out for yourself." Unwilling to miss his reaction, she covered her face with her hands. "I'm not moving away, but I have my eyes closed and I'm not looking."

There was a moment of silence, then that heavy tread on the stairs and her skin prickled. She could almost feel him below her, feel him looking up at her, and the knowledge was suddenly, surprisingly erotic. Her hands were raised to cover her eyes, and she suddenly realized that the position thrust her breasts forward as if displaying them for his gaze. Her nipples tingled, thrusting against the thin cloth of her dress. There was another creak on the stairs, as if he put his foot on the first step of the upper set, but then it was gone, and she felt the weight of his gaze shift.

"Cookies? You made me cookies?"

"You said you liked them. I didn't have all the ingredients, but I did the best I could."

He groaned, a low, deep sound that she felt through her entire body.

"They're delicious."

"As good as Nelly's?" She couldn't help asking.

"Much, much better."

"You know, if you came up here I could teach you how to make cookies, just as you could teach me to play the instrument."

"I..."

"Just think about it," she said quickly. "Now it's been a long day and I'm going to take a bath, so unless you're going to join me, you better move away."

There was a startled intake of breath, and she realized what she said.

"Join me up here, I meant," she said quickly, but she knew she was blushing as she rose to her feet. As she went to take her bath, she couldn't help imagining what it would be like if he did join her.

CHAPTER 7

Once more, Frantor found himself clutching the post at the bottom of the stairs. This time, it was not to keep himself upright but to prevent himself from succumbing to her invitation. *She didn't mean it,* he told himself sternly, but it didn't help. He couldn't help imagining her in the big tub he'd installed, her delightfully curved body flushed and glowing and her hand held out to him.

The image was frustratingly vague—if only he'd been able to see more of her. But seeing more of her meant taking the chance that she would also see more of him. That thought was like a wave of cold water, shocking him back to the reality that he would never see her and she would never see him.

But despite that knowledge, he found himself following her movements as she went to the kitchen area and cleaned up before going to the bathing room. He could hear the faint trickle of water as she washed and her pleased sigh as she sank into the hot waters of the tub. He'd installed it because the heat helped to relieve some of his pain and stiffness, but now he'd never be able to enter it again without thinking of her in the same place.

Fuck. He was acting like a lovelorn youth, although even as a youth he'd never been this enthralled by a female. He hadn't been entirely celibate, but he'd always been more focused on his studies than on females. As much as he loved his parents and appreciated the small town where he'd grown up, he'd always known he wouldn't stay.

I'm being foolish, he thought. But that didn't stop him from leaning against the wall, listening to the soft splashes she made as she moved about in the tub. Or stop his cock from throbbing painfully and incessantly. He actually got as far as putting his hand over it before he stopped in appalled horror. *What am I doing?* He had to remember that he was no longer whole. Better if his body had never reawakened. It certainly wouldn't help to succumb to that need.

But although he did his best to ignore his body's demands, he couldn't bring himself to move away, to miss any of her movements as she bathed and dried herself. Afterwards, she walked across the floor and he could tell she was barefoot. Was the rest of her bare as well? Of course not. That would be foolish, and she was not a foolish woman.

"I'm going to bed now. Are you sure you're all right down there?"

"I'm fine."

He knew he sounded curt, but he was afraid to say too much, afraid that his longing and desire would come pouring out.

"All right, if you're sure. Good night, Frantor."

"Good night, Florie," he said, his chest aching.

How long had it been since he'd shared even that simple exchange with anyone?

He listened again as she made her way to his bed, as she slipped between his sheets. Would her fragrance linger on those sheets after she left? Could he preserve her presence even to that small degree? He would do everything he could to save it.

He could tell that she didn't fall asleep immediately, but eventually her breathing settled into the soft rhythm of slumber. He had no intention of following her into sleep. The bed beneath the stairs had no appeal for him. Because his nights were frequently restless, he sometimes rested there during the day when the lingering pain from his injuries became too much for him. But tonight he was far too conscious of his visitor to have any hope of sleeping.

He needed a distraction—did he dare to turn on one of his work lights? *I will be able to hear her coming,* he assured himself, but despite that, his prosthetic hand trembled as he reached for the switch, and he couldn't make himself do it.

Staring at the mechanical fingers, the gleam of metal obvious even in the dim light that made its way down the stairs, a thought occurred to him. He went to the coat rack next to the outer door, digging through his pockets until he found a pair of gloves. He rarely used them, but now he pulled on the left glove. Better. His hands still did not look entirely normal, but the black leather disguised the metal structure just as his sleeve concealed the rest of his arm, and the sight gave him an unexpected boost of confidence.

Once again, he found himself glancing up the stairs. After a brief hesitation, he put on his cloak and pulled the hood all the way over his head, clutching it to his neck with his gloved hand before walking slowly and quietly up the stairs. He was a big male, but he had learned stealth during his time in the war and he moved silently across the room.

Already there were signs of her presence. Clean dishes perched neatly in the rack in the sink while a covered bowl of dough rested on the back of the stove. The remainder of the cookies were arranged on a plate on the table. His chair had been moved, pushed closer to the uncovered window, and he could imagine her perched there looking out at the valley.

The snow had stopped falling for the moment, and his chest ached again at the thought that the storm might be over, that she might leave him. Enough light came through the window, that he could see her lying in the bed, and he drifted closer, unable to stay away. She was even more beautiful than he remembered. She had a lush, tempting mouth that seemed to be smiling even in her sleep. Long dark lashes rested against cheeks flushed with sleep, and he almost wished that they would open, that he would see her eyes. The bedclothes had slipped down, not far, but far enough for him to see the smooth skin of her throat and the upper swell of her generous breasts beneath the thin white garment she was wearing. Her exposed skin looked bare and tempting and... vulnerable.

He found himself reaching for the covers, pulling them up close around her neck. As he did, she shifted in her sleep and his fingers brushed against her neck, her skin impossibly smooth and soft beneath his hand. So different from his own. He froze, unable to tear his hand away. How long had it been since he had touched another person?

Her eyelids fluttered open, and for just a second she seemed to stare straight at him. Before he could panic, her eyes closed again and she nestled into her pillow with a contented sigh, those luscious lips curving into a smile.

He carefully drew his hand away, his heart pounding as hard as if he'd been about to go into battle, and fled for the safety of his workroom, barely remembering to keep his steps silent.

But once he was back in his sanctuary, he found himself pacing, clutching the hand that had touched her against his chest as if he could preserve that fleeting touch. It had been a mistake to go upstairs, a mistake to see her, let alone touch her. That one interaction had left him hungry for more. But he didn't just want to see her sleeping. He wanted her awake and talking to him, even smiling at him. But how could he take the chance?

As soon as he had stopped clutching the hood of his cloak it had slipped down, revealing his face. He slammed his fist against the wall in frustration, then stopped. He had used his gloved hand, and really, it looked no different than any other hand. If he could disguise his hand, was there also a way to disguise his face? Metal would provide a more permanent solution, but he didn't have the facilities for that. He could carve something out of wood, but that too would not be a rapid process. He trailed his hand across his supply cabinets, thinking. He did have bandages and plaster. It would be a temporary solution, but it only needed to last for the brief, precious time she would be with him.

His heart beating rapidly, he turned on one small light in the far corner of the workroom, pulled out his supplies, and set to work.

CHAPTER 8

Florie had been dreaming—a delicious and decidedly erotic dream about a big cloaked male watching her—and she woke with a smile on her face. A smile on her face and an ache of desire between her legs. In her dream, all she'd been able to see was the male's eyes, dark and mysterious, but it didn't take much imagination to realize that she had been dreaming about Frantor. Her nipples stiffened as she remembered the way he had watched her in her dream.

Would he watch her the same way in real life? She slid her hands down over her aching breasts as she imagined his eyes following them. The taut peaks throbbed under her gentle touch, surprising her. Sex with Mathew hadn't been unpleasant exactly, but neither had it been satisfying. She certainly couldn't remember her body ever responding to his touch this way, let alone to the mere thought of him. There had been no one since then—until now. Somehow her long neglected libido had been awakened by the mysterious, tortured male hiding in the darkness below.

The thought of Frantor sent another odd little quiver of desire through her body and her hands started to tighten on her breasts, but then she heard movement from below. Even though she knew he wouldn't come upstairs, she jumped. Time to get up. She had slept in her chemise, but she quickly fastened her corset, then pulled her dress back over her head with a sigh.

"You'd think if someone was going to abduct me, he could have been thoughtful enough to bring me some clothes," she muttered to herself.

"Did you say something?"

That deep, beautiful voice made her still hardened nipples tingle, and she knew she was blushing as she moved to the top of the stairs.

"Just bemoaning my limited wardrobe. I'll get started on breakfast."

"You are welcome to any of my clothing if it would be helpful."

Why did the thought of wearing his clothes seem so appealing—and so unexpectedly erotic?

"Thank you," she said, trying not to sound breathless. "I hope it won't be necessary. Do you think the storm will end soon?"

"It stopped for a while during the night, but it seems to be back to full intensity this morning."

She looked over at the uncovered window and realized that he was right. The outside world was almost completely obscured by a cloud of white. And yet she didn't feel as upset about it as she probably should have. At some point during the previous day, she had accepted that her life was on hold for now, and she was in no hurry to return to it.

She also realized guiltily that she hadn't closed the curtain on the window.

"Do you want me to close the curtains again?"

There was a long silence.

"No," he said finally. "I thought perhaps…"

His voice died away.

"You thought perhaps what?"

"I thought I might join you for the meal. If that would not alarm you," he added quickly.

"Alarm me?" Her heart was pounding, but she didn't think it was from fear. "I wouldn't be alarmed."

"I am not as other males."

Her heart melted at the despair in his voice.

"Maybe that's an advantage," she said firmly. "I'll get started on breakfast. You come and join me whenever you're ready."

She checked on the dough she'd left to rise, then turned it out and kneaded it quickly before placing it in the loaf pan she had found. Once it was in the oven, she started frying some slices of ham. She was turning them over when she heard the slow footsteps coming up the stairs. Her heart was beating wildly, but she kept her focus on the meat.

"Just have a seat. This will be ready in a minute," she said as casually as possible.

"I think perhaps you should decide if you are willing to share a meal with me first. Turn around, Florie."

She slowly obeyed, her pulse racing.

He was standing at the top of the stairs, and her memory had not betrayed her, he was just as large as she had remembered, his presence dominating the room. Despite the warmth of the room, he was still wearing the dark cloak that concealed his body, the hood drawn forward over his head. The garment seemed to amplify the width of his broad shoulders and his powerful frame. Under the shadow of the hood, his face looked oddly smooth and white. His hand clenched on the stair railing as she looked at him and she realized it was covered by a black glove. The wood creaked as his grip tightened.

The tension revealed by that tight grip was oddly reassuring and she smiled at him.

"Are you going to come and sit down?"

"You are not afraid?"

"Of course not. You told me you wouldn't hurt me."

"Never," he said immediately. "What I meant was my... my appearance."

"All I can really see is a cloak," she pointed out. "Why don't you take it off? Only if you want to," she added hastily.

His body grew even stiffer.

"Don't be afraid," he whispered finally, and pushed back the hood of his cloak.

It took a moment for her to realize what she was seeing. The odd whiteness she had seen under his hood was a plaster mask, one that extended from his forehead to just beneath his cheeks, dark eyes glittering behind the eye openings. The mask left his mouth uncovered—a full, sensual mouth with the slightest twist at one corner, pulled up by a scar that disappeared under the edge of his mask.

The white of the mask was a striking contrast to the pale bluish green of his skin. Thick dark hair tumbled over the top of the mask, reaching almost to his eyes, and she had the sudden impulse to smooth it back, to put her hand on his face and tell him that everything was fine.

"Well, come and sit down," she said, turning back to the cookstove. "You don't want your food to get cold."

She waited, half-expecting him to disappear back down the stairs, but instead she heard him cross over to the table and sit.

CHAPTER 9

Frantor clung to the stair railing a moment longer, his knees weak with relief. It had taken more courage to push back his hood than it had to face even the worst battle. There were no mirrors in the workroom, but he had checked and rechecked his makeshift mask a dozen times, running his fingers along the edge over and over to make sure that the majority of his facial scars were concealed. Even now, he checked one more time and then made sure that the straps tied around his head were still firmly in place.

He'd been tempted to keep his hood up, but in the end he decided that if she could not accept his disguise, he'd rather know now—before he became accustomed to being in her presence. When her eyes widened he tensed, waiting for any sign of horror but she didn't look afraid. Indeed, as her eyes drifted down over the rest of him, she almost looked... appreciative. It was impossible of course, but that memory gave him the courage to finally release the railing and move to the table, sinking down in his chair with a sigh of relief before he remembered that he only had the one chair. Although his brothers occasionally visited him, they never came beyond the workshop, and he had never expected to have anyone else here in his sanctuary.

"You should sit," he said, rising to his feet immediately.

"I don't mind. I'm used to running around waiting on people."

"I do not want you to wait on me."

The words came out harsher than he intended and she gave him a startled look.

"I do not think of you as a servant," he added.

"That's good because I don't think of myself that way either. Why would you—oh, I get it. That's what Nelly was worried about, wasn't it?"

He hesitated, then nodded. The memory of Nelly's fears had been a factor, but not the only one. He wanted her to think of him as a… companion, not a chore, but he wasn't sure how to express the sentiment.

She tapped her finger thoughtfully on those luscious lips of hers, and he couldn't look away. What would it be like to touch that soft pink flesh? He was so entranced by the prospect that it took him a moment to realize she was looking at him expectantly.

"I'm sorry. What did you say?"

She smiled, seemingly undisturbed by his distraction.

"I said there are some barrels in the pantry. If you bring one of them out here, I could use that as a seat."

He thought about it for a moment, then decided it was an acceptable solution.

"Very well, but I will be the one to use it."

"If you insist. Why don't you do that while I get the bread out of the oven?"

The barrel closest to the door was almost full of flour, but it was easy enough for him to move. As he carried it over to the table, she shot him another glance and this time he was quite sure it was admiring.

"You're very strong, aren't you?"

"I suppose so. All of my brothers are—we are warriors."

"Even now?" she asked softly as she brought the warm bread to the table.

"Always, I think. Battle changes you."

She reached across the table and for the barest second, her hand covered his.

"I'm sorry you had to go through that."

His hand tingled, the skin on fire with sensation as if she had touched him with a burning brand instead of her naked flesh. He couldn't move.

"What's wrong?" she asked softly. "Did I upset you?"

"No," he barked, then did his best to modulate his voice. "It has just been a... long time since anyone touched me."

She looked at him across the table, her green eyes clear and knowing. "It's been a long time since I touched a man."

"I am not a man."

She didn't seem offended by his immediate denial, smiling at him.

"All right, a male. Is that better?"

Before she came, he might have denied it, might have argued that he was no longer even that, but with his cock throbbing incessantly, it was impossible to argue.

"What are your people called?"

"We are Riasi, from the planet Vizal."

"And that's where the war was fought?"

"Yes, but it was not our war. Two different political coalitions claimed our planet. They fought back and forth across our planet for ten years. In the end, the politicians reached an agreement and they simply walked away from the damage they had caused, leaving behind a destroyed planet."

"Is that why you left?"

"I no longer belonged there," he said shortly. It was true, for many reasons. "Artek and our squad are my family now."

"I see," she said, then smiled at him. "Maybe that's enough talk about the past. Although it doesn't seem to have affected your appetite," she added, looking at his plate.

He ducked his head, embarrassed by his gluttony.

"It has been a long time since I have had fresh bread. It was delicious."

She smiled again, obviously pleased.

"I meant what I said before. I'd be happy to teach you to cook. Bread isn't particularly difficult."

"I suspect that's easy to say with your experience."

She laughed as she pushed back her chair and stood, gathering their plates.

"Probably. But I managed to teach Roger. My assistant," she added.

"Since you cooked, I should clean."

Her gaze dropped to his gloved hand, and she shook her head.

"I really don't mind."

Fuck. He didn't want her treating him as an invalid or an object of pity. His prosthetic hand was not natural, but he didn't think it was disgusting. She had accepted the mask—could she accept his hand as well? He took a deep breath, and then he pulled off the glove.

"My hand is not disabled. It is a mechanical replacement."

"Really? That's fascinating." She started to reach for his hand, then hesitated, looking up at him. "May I?"

He nodded, unable to speak, and she took his artificial hand in hers. It was the most basic of models—a simple metal structure that replaced his missing hand and did an adequate job of mimicking the normal motions of his hand. It could return her grasp, and he did so, closing the metal fingers delicately around her hand, wishing that he had the ability to feel her skin.

"That's amazing. Can you feel my hand?" she asked, unconsciously mimicking his thoughts.

"Not exactly. I know that your hand is there and I can apply and release pressure." He squeezed her hand very, very gently.

"But this model does not allow me to feel sensation the way skin feels sensation."

"That's a shame," she said softly, leaving her hand in his.

He saw her looking at where the metal structure disappeared beneath his sleeve and then up the length of his arm.

"It extends all the way to my shoulder," he said, and she gave him a guilty look.

"I wasn't going to ask."

"I know. Maybe that's why I told you."

She smiled at him, and he actually found himself smiling back. The unfamiliar expression pulled on the scar at the corner of his mouth, reminding him that his arm was far from the worst of his injuries. Just because she seemed to have accepted it did not mean that she would accept the rest of him—yet looking at her hand intertwined with his metal fingers gave him an unexpected feeling of hope.

Her fingers were long and graceful, but strong and roughened by work. Despite the difference in size, they looked… right intertwined with his.

Greatly daring, he put his other hand briefly over hers.

"Thank you."

"For what? For breakfast?"

"Yes, but also for this. For not being afraid."

"I'm not afraid of you, Frantor," she said, looking directly at his face, her gaze clear and unflinching. She squeezed his hand one more time, then rose.

"Now... how about if I wash the dishes and you tune up the zinar? Let's see if you can teach me to produce something that doesn't sound like a dying animal."

He found himself smiling again—and this time it didn't feel quite so strange.

CHAPTER 10

Florie heard the scrape of the barrel being pushed back from the table, then nothing else. Was he still standing there watching her? The fine hairs on the back of her neck prickled at the thought, and she had to clench the dish she was washing to avoid reaching back and smoothing her dress down over her butt. She didn't dislike the idea of him watching her—on the contrary, she wished she could do the same. Why did he insist on staying covered? His size was undeniable, as was his strength, but she would like to have seen more of him. She would even have liked him to remove his mask, but if it made him feel more comfortable, she would never ask. Perhaps in time he would come to trust her enough to do it on his own.

She still didn't hear the sound of footsteps, but then the light, tinkling notes of the zinar began to fill the room. It wasn't a recognizable tune, just a series of notes, but she smiled as she finished the last of the dishes and turned towards him. He was sitting in the big chair, his naked hand moving easily between the two necks while his metal fingers plucked at the strings.

"Have you always played?" she asked as she went to join him, admiring the ease with which he manipulated the strings.

She had a sudden vision of those agile fingers dancing across her own body, the resulting rush of desire taking her by surprise. Where had the sudden awakening come from? But as Frantor looked up and their eyes met, she knew. This scarred, wounded male called to her in a way she'd never felt before.

His eyes remained fixed on hers, dark and mysterious behind the mask, and she took a half-step closer before she reconsidered. Her movement broke the spell. He jerked and started to rise. She saw a slight, betraying flinch as he climbed to his feet, the knuckles whitening on his bare hand as he used the arm of the chair to assist him.

"Are you all right?"

"Fine," he barked, then slowly shook his head. "My leg stiffens when it is tired."

Guilt immediately swamped her.

"I knew I shouldn't have taken your bed. You can sleep up here tonight, and I'll sleep downstairs in the workroom."

"Absolutely not."

"Why not? It would be just fine for me."

"The workroom is no place for a delicate female," he growled.

She put her hands on her hips and glared at him. "First of all, I am not a delicate female. Second of all, women are perfectly capable in a workroom. Not that I'm particularly mechanical," she added quickly. "But the kitchen is my workroom and I work damn hard."

"I meant no disrespect. But that space is cool and dark—you would not like that. You belong up here in the light." He looked at the curtains covering all the windows except the one next to the bed. "You should open the rest of the curtains, let in the light."

"Won't that make you uncomfortable?"

"No more uncomfortable than I have been so far," he said dryly, and her quick spurt of anger disappeared.

"At least think about letting me sleep in the workroom. I really hate the idea that you're hurting because of me. Or maybe we could take turns?"

"I assure you I would be far less comfortable up here knowing you were downstairs in the workroom."

Those dark eyes were fixed on her face again, and she realized that their bodies were only a short distance apart. All she would have to do would be to take one step forward and she would almost be touching him. Perhaps some evidence of her thought appeared on her face because he suddenly stepped to one side, his left leg dragging slightly, and a new thought occurred to her.

"Is your leg also prosthetic?" she blurted out.

He had partially turned away from her, but she could see the tension in that massive back as he slowly shook his head.

"I am... scarred."

This time, she did step forward, placing her hand lightly on his back. Warmth spread from that slight contact, her fingers tingling as she felt the hard, warm muscles beneath the cloak. And then he was gone, moving to the top of the stairs with a speed that belied his injuries.

"Please do not touch me."

His voice sounded tortured, and once again she was overwhelmed by guilt.

"I'm sorry. I didn't mean to hurt you."

He paused for a fraction of a second.

"You did not cause me pain."

He disappeared down the stairs, leaving her staring after him with her mouth open. If she hadn't hurt him, why had he been in such a hurry to leave? But then she realized that her fingers were still tingling from the contact and her nipples were throbbing against her dress. *Oh.* A slow smile unexpectedly curved her lips.

It's probably only because he isn't used to being around women, she thought, but after so many years of being casually glanced at and then dismissed, his apparent desire was an unexpected balm.

"Will you come back up for lunch?" she called downstairs. "I'll make more cookies," she added.

It hadn't escaped her notice that the remainder of the plate of cookies had disappeared during their breakfast.

"Perhaps."

His deep voice sounded hesitant, but she refused to let that deter her. She returned to the pantry, determined to find something impossible for him to resist. She knew he had a sweet tooth and that he enjoyed bread. She found a container of dried fruit and nodded with satisfaction. She could make bread pudding with the remains of this morning's loaf. She didn't have fresh eggs, but there was a large container of powdered egg substitute that should work. She mixed the ingredients and set it to one side so that the bread could absorb the liquid while she considered the problem of lunch.

After another survey of the pantry, she decided to make chili. The working men who came to her diner always enjoyed it, and hopefully the smell of it would be enticing enough to lure him up the stairs. He had all the ingredients she needed, and she wondered once again why he had so many supplies when he didn't cook.

Once the chili was simmering away on the back of the stove, she found herself wandering restlessly around the room once again. While it was a pleasant change from the long hours of hard work at the diner, she wasn't used to being idle. Between planning menus and cooking and ordering supplies, there was always something to be done, and the diner itself saw a constant stream of activity. Even on a slow afternoon, Nelly or one of her other friends would frequently stop by for a pot of tea and some friendly gossip about all the latest goings-on in town.

She ended up at the top of the stairs again. There were lights on below and she could hear the sound of movement.

"What are you doing down there?"

"Working."

She refused to let the brief answer discourage her.

"What are you working on? Is there anything I can do to help?"

"You want to help me?"

"Yes. I'm kind of bored up here by myself."

The resulting silence was so long that she started to move away from the stairs, but then he gave what sounded like a muffled groan.

"All right. You may come down."

She skipped eagerly down the stairs. A bright light shone down on one of the work tables, and he was standing beside it, still wrapped in his cloak, the hood pulled up over his head once more.

"You really don't have to wear that because of me."

She caught a brief flash of his eyes before he looked away, shaking his head.

"I prefer to wear it."

She bit back a sigh and moved closer, stopping an arm's length away.

"What are you working on?"

He picked up a small metal device with a rectangular body and delicate wings that looked like some kind of oversized metal insect, then glanced at her from under his hood.

"When you arrived, I did not know that you were here."

"That was pretty obvious," she said dryly. "But it must have been dark and snowing when I was... left for you."

"That should not have made a difference. I have been softened by this easy life."

She couldn't help it, she snorted.

"I can't think of anyone less soft—and I mean that in a good way," she added quickly when she saw his hand tense.

His head turned towards her once more, and she saw his eyes gleaming mysteriously in the depths of the hood. Tension simmered between them, and she waited breathlessly for his response, but in the end he simply turned back to his device.

"I'm creating drones that I can send out across the ranch to alert me of strangers."

"So you can get away before another woman shows up on your doorstep?"

The question came out harsher than she intended, but the knowledge that her presence made him more determined to avoid people stung.

To her shock, his hand reached out and covered hers where it was clenched at her side.

"That is not what I meant. You will always be welcome here. But although your appearance was a... delightful surprise, you could have been an enemy instead."

"Delightful?" she whispered, turning her hand over so that her fingers could clasp his.

"Yes," he said firmly. "Not easy, perhaps, but delightful nonetheless."

She stared up at him, wishing she could really see him, and then the rest of his words penetrated. An enemy? Here?

"Who do you expect to attack you?"

"I don't know, but I have learned to expect the unexpected. It is better to be prepared."

Her heart ached at the pain in that deep, beautiful voice. She wanted to reassure him that he was safe, but she suspected her words would not be enough to convince him. Instead, she squeezed his hand, then reluctantly disentangled her fingers.

"Then show me what I can do to help."

CHAPTER 11

As soon as Florie went upstairs to check on her lunch preparations, Frantor collapsed on the mattress in the alcove beneath the stairs. His legs were actually trembling. The weakness was partially physical—he hadn't slept the previous night, and he was unused to spending several hours on his feet. But his injuries were only partially responsible for his weakened state. Having Florie with him in the workroom had been as delightful as he told her—delightful and torturous.

She had insisted on staying and helping him. She was right— she wasn't a mechanic—but she had agile fingers and she learned quickly. It certainly wasn't her fault that he'd been mesmerized watching those agile hands manipulating the small pieces of metal. He couldn't help but imagine her touching him with those same delicate touches. Thank the gods that he had kept his cloak on. The long folds concealed the massive erection that even now was pressed painfully against his pants. He'd never realized it was possible to be so hopelessly aroused for such an extended period of time.

Several times their hands accidentally touched, sending a renewed jolt of lust through his system, and once they had both reached for the same part at the same time and their bodies had collided. They had only been in contact for an instant, but he'd almost erupted just from the feel of those lush curves pressed against his body. He had been so focused on trying to control himself that it had taken him a moment to notice that her cheeks were flushed as she turned away and that the sweetness of her scent had increased. He wanted so desperately to believe that she had also been aroused by that contact, but he was sure that it was only the momentary proximity of their bodies.

He could hear her moving around upstairs, humming softly as she prepared a meal for him—for them. He already knew that despite his earlier words, he would be joining her. He would join her whenever she asked. He knew it would only make her inevitable departure that much more agonizing—but then he had a lot of experience with agony. At least this time it would be preceded by pleasure. Perhaps she would even touch him again…

At the thought, his cock jerked and he fisted it impatiently. He couldn't walk around in a permanent state of arousal. Keeping a wary eye on the stairs, he freed his erection, almost groaning with relief as it escaped the tight confines of the fabric.

"Is anything wrong, Frantor?"

Florie's sweet voice floated down the stairs, but she didn't come down.

"No," he managed to say, even as he closed his hand around his cock.

"All right. Lunch will be ready in a few minutes."

He couldn't manage a reply, but he heard her move away. The knowledge that she was so close made him even harder. What if she had come down the stairs and seen him exposed this way? Would she have run away in horror? Would she have put those long supple fingers around his shaft, stroking him with the same firm touch she'd used to assemble the drones? He stroked himself, imagining that it was her hand, imagining that she was looking up at him with those clear green eyes, those luscious lips parted. Imagining that she would place them around his cock and draw him into the sweet haven of her mouth.

"Are you coming?"

And at the sound of her voice, he did, his seed erupting in great creamy spurts that splashed across his stomach and chest as his body shuddered helplessly. He was still gasping for breath when she spoke again.

"Are you sure you're all right? Do you want me to come down?"

"No!" He took a deep breath and managed to modulate his voice. "I'll be there in a minute. I just need to... clean up."

He could hear the ragged note in his voice, but after a brief pause, she moved away again.

"Whenever you're ready."

He forced himself to his feet, wincing when his leg twinged as he stood. He ignored it, limping to the small facility at the back of the workroom. Part of him was still shocked by how quickly and violently he had climaxed, but there was also a certain satisfaction in the realization that at least that part of him was fully functional. A satisfaction that lasted until he removed his damp shirt and looked down at the ruin of his body. At the inflamed ridges where his prosthetic was attached to his shoulder and the scars that twisted his flesh all the way down the left side of his body. He was not a male; he was a monster. How could he even imagine that a beautiful female like Florie would ever want to touch him?

He pulled on a clean shirt, making sure it was fastened all the way to the neck before donning his cloak again. He shouldn't even think of joining her for the meal, but he suspected that if he did not, she would be concerned enough to come and find him. The last thing he wanted was for her to think of him as an object of pity. No, he would simply eat and then return to the workroom. Alone.

His resolve began to fade as soon as he climbed the stairs and found her waiting for him. By the table. She smiled as if she were genuinely glad to see him, but then her head tilted.

"You put your hood back up."

It had fallen down twice while he was working, and eventually he had given up and just left it down since it didn't seem to bother her. She actually seemed disappointed now, but he felt the need for its protection.

"That looks good," he said, ignoring her remark.

"It's just chili and cornbread, but I hope you'll like it." Her eyes twinkled. "If you're a good boy and finish it all, I also made bread pudding for dessert."

"That sounds... interesting."

She laughed as she handed him a large bowl of food and placed a platter of golden squares on the table between them.

"I'm sure you'll like it."

"I like everything you cook." He groaned his approval as the succulent, spicy meat filled his mouth. "This is excellent."

Her cheeks flushed pink, the same pink they had turned when their bodies touched earlier, but she looked pleased.

"Thank you. I do enjoy cooking and it's nice to have all the ingredients." She shot him a glance as she took a spoonful from her much smaller bowl. "Your pantry is so well stocked, especially for someone who doesn't know how to cook. I've never seen such a variety of fruits and vegetables."

"Gilmat has a huge garden, and a talent for growing things."

"I can tell. But it still seems like a lot of food. Were you... expecting someone to join you?"

The sound that emerged from his lips was too bitter to be called a laugh.

"Never. I just thought that perhaps I could learn. I listened sometimes as Nelly explained to Benjar what she was doing, but my own experiments were never successful."

And he'd quickly realized that it wasn't just the food he wanted —he missed the companionship of his brothers.

"It really helps to have someone there showing you what to do. I'm sure I can teach you."

"I would be happy to learn." Anything she wished to teach him.

"But maybe we could try a music lesson first?"

Her voice was gently teasing, but he suspected that if his skin could change colors the way that hers did, it would darken at the memory of the way he had fled.

"Very well."

To his relief, she smiled at his assent and changed the subject. He told her more about his plans for the drones as they ate, carefully avoiding any mention of how he had previously employed them during the war. He ate far too much of her delicious food, including the bread pudding which was as delightful as she had promised. By the time the meal ended, he was feeling more content than he'd thought possible.

"We'll just leave the dishes for now," she said cheerfully as they finished and rose from the table. "Where do you want me?"

In my bed. It took all his strength not to glance at the bed in the corner. Instead, he pointed at the chair.

"You will sit. I will bring my barrel," he added to forestall her protest.

He picked it up and carried it over next to the chair, but as he put it down disaster struck. His leg cramped, sending a fiery streak of agony through his body as he swayed. Florie immediately pushed him down into the chair, and he was too busy trying not to scream to object.

"What is it? Is it your leg?"

He couldn't answer, all of his muscles locked tight as wave after wave of pain washed over him. His hands clenched so tightly on the arms of the chair that he was distantly aware that the one beneath his metal hand cracked. It wasn't the first time this had happened. He knew that all he could do was wait it out, but the muscles in his legs began to relax much quicker than normal. It took him far longer than it should have done to realize that she was touching him, her hands kneading the rigid muscles in his calf and thigh and helping them to loosen.

His eyes flew open, and he looked down to find her kneeling between his legs. She smiled up at him as her hands worked their way further up his thigh.

"Good. It looks like this is helping."

At the sight of her smiling up at him from between his legs, his erection came roaring back, his shaft swelling helplessly just as her hands reached his upper thigh. Her fingers brushed against it once, then again, and then her hand stilled and she looked up at him, her eyes wide and her lips parted just as they had been in his imagination.

CHAPTER 12

Florie was so intent on loosening the tight muscles in Frantor's leg that it took her a moment to realize that the hard bar brushing against her fingers was not simply another rigid muscle. He was erect—massively erect. She looked up and saw his eyes closed in what looked like despair, and she quickly snatched her hand away, even though she longed to linger and explore. But despite her embarrassment, she kept massaging his thigh.

"You don't have to keep doing that."

His deep voice was strained, but he didn't push her hands away so she kept going. She did her best to focus on her movements, but her eyes couldn't help straying to that enormous erection. Given his overall size, it wasn't entirely surprising that he would be well endowed, but damn he was big. Was it the same as a human cock, she wondered. And why did she suddenly want so desperately to find out?

When their bodies had collided earlier, she had been overwhelmingly conscious of the size and strength of his body. It had excited her, just as looking at him excited her now. Her breasts felt swollen and achy, and there was a low pulse of desire between her legs.

Don't be ridiculous, she told herself. It wasn't as if there was a future for them. She would never see him again once the storm ended. He'd made it quite clear that he didn't welcome visitors, and she certainly couldn't see him coming to town.

His prosthetic hand closed over hers, and she realized with a start that she had almost stopped moving as her thoughts wandered.

"It's better now. Thank you."

She looked down at her hand, almost delicate-looking against the thick muscles of his thigh, at his metal fingers holding her in place, and she shivered, but it was a shiver of excitement. From the way he immediately snatched his hand away, she suspected he misinterpreted it.

"I'm fine," he said stiffly.

"I know you are." She deliberately gave his thigh a quick squeeze as she smiled up at him. "Does this happen often?"

His mouth was drawn tight, the sensuous lips pressed together.

"Sometimes. When I have forgotten that I am no longer the male I once was."

Ignoring the bitterness in his voice, she squeezed his leg again, doing her best to ignore the way his cock jerked at her touch.

"What do you do when you're by yourself?"

"I'm always by myself." He hesitated, then shrugged a shoulder. "The bath helps."

"That makes sense. The heat and the movement of the water would be like a massage." She gave his thigh a last pat and rose, brushing off her skirts.

"I think you should go and take a bath now. It should help with any lingering stiffness."

"A bath?"

He sounded as appalled as if she had suggested he throw himself into the icy river, and it took her a moment to understand why.

"I promise you, you're safe. I won't open the door."

His eyes looked so vulnerable behind the mask that she gave into temptation and leaned forward, brushing a quick kiss to his uncovered mouth.

"You're safe with me," she repeated, then fled to the kitchen area.

She deliberately kept her back turned as she started gathering up their lunch dishes. She heard him stand, and her heart skipped a beat. Was he going to escape back downstairs? She didn't hear any more footsteps, but then she heard the bathroom door close and sighed with relief. She wasn't quite sure why it was so important that he trust her enough to do this, but it really meant a lot that he had.

Even though she tried to concentrate on the dishes, she found herself listening for what seemed like an inordinate length of time before she finally heard the sound of water and knew he had entered the tub. Her relief was immediately followed by a pulse of arousal at the thought of his huge naked body only a short distance away.

She would never betray his trust, but she suddenly wished that she were in there with him. She knew that he was badly scarred. Not only had he told her so but as she massaged his leg, she had felt the ridges of scar tissue, so many ridges. Although her heart ached at the pain he must have endured, the knowledge that he was scarred did not bother her.

Based on the size of his erection, he was as attracted to her as she was to him. Could she persuade him to explore the attraction between them further? She knew it would be difficult, and the last thing she wanted to do was to hurt him, but why couldn't they have this time together, however brief?

She put the last dish on the rack to dry, then wiped her hands and wandered over to the window. The snow was falling as heavily as ever and showed no signs of letting up. They still had time. But she was going to have to be the one to make the move. She'd never fancied herself as a seductress, but she found the thought rather intriguing. She would never do anything that Frantor didn't want, but she could certainly encourage him to admit what he did want.

When he finally emerged from the bathroom, she gave him a quick assessing look from under her lashes. His mouth had relaxed, no longer drawn in that taut line. He was moving more easily, walking across the room with that quick, silent gait. He'd put his cloak back on, but he left the hood down and a lock of dark hair fell down across one side of his mask. Once again, she had the urge to smooth it back, to see if it felt as soft as it looked.

He hesitated by the table, and she looked up from the potatoes she'd been peeling and gave him a teasing smile.

"Don't think you've gotten out of our music lesson. I'm still determined to learn how to play."

"I... I intended to do some more work on the drones."

"Can't they wait a little bit longer? I'd be happy to help."

"I suppose."

"Good."

She carried the potatoes to the sink, put them in a bowl of cold water, and washed her hands. When she turned back, he was still standing uncertainly by the table.

"I was thinking about this while you were bathing, and I have a better idea."

She took his hand, ignoring the way his breath caught, and led him to the bed.

CHAPTER 13

Frantor knew he should pull his hand away, knew that he shouldn't be following her over to the bed. His pulse was thudding so rapidly in his ears that he could barely hear what she was saying as she came to a halt next to the bed. He was so busy remembering the way she had looked sleeping there and trying to get his body under control that it took him a moment to realize that the zinar was lying on the bed.

"Sit down," she said, and he had a feeling it wasn't for the first time. She had followed her own instructions, and tugged gently at his hand as she gave him a sunny smile.

"This will be much easier for you to show me how to play."

She didn't have the strength to compel him, and yet he could no more resist that gentle tug than he could stop breathing. As he sat next to her, the mattress sagged a little, pushing the sides of their bodies together. He could feel every inch of that contact like a burning brand running from his shoulder to his hip.

"Now what do I do?"

The question was innocent enough, but there was a husky note to her voice that promised so much more. Could she possibly be... flirting with him? He dismissed the idea immediately. She was just being nice. He only hoped it wasn't because she pitied him. The thought made him stiffen, and his voice came out gruffly as he pointed to the instrument.

"Pick it up and place it across your lap, angling the necks back towards your shoulder."

She looked a little startled at his abruptness, but she obeyed. When she had the zinar in place, he tried unsuccessfully to explain how to position her fingers on the strings. He took the instrument away and demonstrated before returning it to her. Her second attempt was better, but she still didn't quite have it. This time, he placed his fingers over hers, adjusting their position.

Even this minimal touch thrilled him and he found himself reluctant to move his hand away. She didn't complain, letting him move her fingers beneath his as she brushed her thumb slowly across the strings. The note was a little shaky, but a definite improvement on the discordant sounds she'd made previously and she gave him a triumphant smile.

"I knew we could do it. Please show me more."

How could he resist?

He walked her through one of the simple songs he remembered from his childhood. It took several attempts, and at one point he found himself with both arms around her as he guided her fingers on the necks of the zinar while showing her how to pluck the strings with her other hand. Their closeness had the inevitable effect on his body and his cock was painfully stiff when he moved away.

"You should have it now. Try the whole thing."

Her cheeks were pink again, and he wondered if she felt the evidence of his desire, but she simply bent over the instrument, her beautiful face determined. She managed to make it through the whole tune, if somewhat roughly, and immediately repeated it a second time. The second time was more successful, and she beamed at him.

"I've always wanted to learn to play a musical instrument."

"Why didn't you?"

"I told you my aunt raised me. She thought it was frivolous."

"Music is never frivolous."

"I agree, but I think she really thought she was doing what was best for me." She shrugged. "And then after I left home, I never really had a chance to learn. Did you learn as a child?"

His chest suddenly ached, and he looked away from her. His earliest memories were of his mother singing. Music had always been a part of his life. Everything from the ritual songs that celebrated the turns of the seasons to bawdy songs with his friends as soon as he was old enough to visit the local tavern.

"Yes. Music is important in Riasi culture. My parents would have been happy if I'd chosen to become a musician."

"But that wasn't what you wanted?"

"As much as I enjoyed it, I was more fascinated by how things worked."

If his first memory was of his mother singing, his second was of her walking in on him as he dismantled her cleaning machine. And her shock when he managed to put it back together. He shook his head.

"I was always taking things apart, but I usually managed to get them together again. Even if there were occasionally a few parts left over."

She laughed and ran a gentle finger across the strings.

"Are there words to go with this?"

"Yes, but they are in my language."

"I don't mind. Will you sing while I play?"

How long had it been since he had sung for anyone other than himself? But oh, how he wanted to. He gave an abrupt nod, and she began to play. It was a simple song about a shepherd and his flock and he'd sung it hundreds of times over the years, but as his voice floated out into the room, memories surrounded him. Not painful memories but joyous ones, their pleasure enhanced by the beautiful female sitting next to him and bending so diligently over the instrument.

Her timing was far from perfect, but he adapted to her more hesitant pace and they finished more or less together, the last note dying away into the silence of the big room. She looked up at him with a delighted smile.

"That was wonderful. You have a beautiful voice."

She put the instrument down and rose to her feet. Even sitting he was tall enough that their faces were almost on a level. She looked at him for a long moment, her face soft, and still caught up in the pleasure of making music together, for once he didn't feel the need to flinch away.

And then she leaned forward and kissed him. Unlike the previous time, this was a real kiss. Her luscious mouth pressed against his, warm and soft, and he felt the teasing flick of her tongue against his lips. His entire body shuddered, and his self-control vanished. He pulled her hard against him, groaning as their bodies came together. She gave a soft squeak of surprise, and he used the opportunity to force her lips apart, determined to devour every drop of her sweetness as he explored her mouth.

Her arms circled his neck as she returned his kiss with equal passion. He could feel the hard peaks of her nipples rubbing against his chest despite the fabric separating them and smell the increased sweetness of her arousal. He pulled her even closer, enthralled by their closeness, by the luscious softness of her body against his.

She writhed against him and one of her hands went to his head, gripping his hair as she tried to pull him even closer. But as she did, he felt his mask shift, just the tiniest bit, but fear turned the blood in his veins to ice. If the mask came loose... If she saw him as he really was... All of his deficiencies came rushing back and he seized her by the waist, pushing her away so that he could stand. Even then, his hands wanted to linger on her skin, but he forced himself to drop them and step away from her.

"I apologize," he said stiffly.

She looked up at him, her eyes huge and dark. Her lips were red and swollen and her cheeks flushed.

"Why are you apologizing? I kissed you."

"You shouldn't have done it. I am no longer a whole male."

"Frantor…"

Her hand reached for him, but he couldn't take it, couldn't allow himself to forget again.

"I have to work. I do not need your help."

The words echoed harshly between them. She looked as if she'd been slapped, and he immediately regretted them. But perhaps it was for the best. Without another word, he turned and headed for the stairs.

CHAPTER 14

Florie stared after Frantor in dismay. His rejection stung for a moment, but then she sighed. She had pushed him too far, too fast. So much for getting him used to her touch. But then she hadn't expected a simple kiss to intensify so rapidly. Certainly no human male had ever inspired such immediate passion. Her cheeks heated as she thought of how shamelessly she had rubbed herself against him, but then again his arousal was equally apparent. And the way he had kissed her... like a drowning man clinging to a lifeline. No one had ever kissed her like that—as if they couldn't exist without her.

Arousal still hummed through her veins, but as much as she had enjoyed their encounter she didn't want to rush him, or scare him off. She would just have to take it slowly with him. She looked thoughtfully at the stairs. Should she just go down and join him as if it had never happened? Or did he need some time to come to terms with their kiss?

Deciding to give him some time, she went to the kitchen and began her dinner preparations—a slow cooked rice dish using meat from the cold locker. While it was cooking, she tried to practice a little more with the zinar, but her fingers were sore from the earlier session. It would take a little time for them to toughen up. Instead she made herself a cup of tea and stared out the window at the falling snow as she considered her options. By the time night had fallen and dinner was ready, she had decided on her approach.

"Frantor," she called down the stairs. "Dinner is ready."

"I'm not hungry."

She wasn't entirely surprised by his response. She returned to the table, loaded everything up on a tray, and started carefully down the stairs. She only made it as far as the landing before he appeared, quickly taking the tray away from her.

"What are you doing? You shouldn't be carrying anything heavy down the stairs. You might fall."

"You didn't want to come to me, so I'm coming to you."

"I told you I wasn't hungry."

Despite the gruffness of his voice, the eyes behind the mask never left her face. She gave him an innocent look.

"Well, I'm hungry, and I don't want to eat by myself, so I decided to come and join you. Of course, if you don't like my cooking…"

She did her best to look sad, and he made an impatient noise.

"You know damn well I like your cooking. I will eat later."

"Then I'll wait and eat with you."

"It might be very late."

"That's fine. It's not like I have anything else to do, all alone upstairs."

He stared at her for a moment, then the corner of his mouth twisted and he gave her that lopsided smile.

"You are a very stubborn woman, aren't you, Florie?"

"Yes, I am. I've found that it's the only way to get what I want."

"All right, you win. I'll bring the tray upstairs, and we will eat together. And then I'm coming back to work," he added sternly.

"If you say so."

"I do, and I mean it."

She simply shrugged and started back up the stairs. He growled and followed her.

The meal went better than she had expected. He was stiff at first, but she coaxed him into talking more about the drones and his plans for them and he gradually relaxed. And despite his professed lack of hunger, he eagerly devoured their meal. They sat talking long after the meal was finished, but eventually he stood and announced he was going back to work.

He said it defiantly, as if he expected her to protest, but she only nodded. He seemed surprised, and possibly even disappointed, and she wished yet again that she could see more of his face. He hesitated for another moment, then returned to the workroom. She gave a silent sigh as she watched him go. She hated thinking of him working into the night, or trying to sleep in the small alcove under the stairs, but she knew she had to give him time.

I'm running out of time.

Florie sighed as she looked out the window. The storm hadn't let up, but over the past few days there had been longer periods when the snow didn't fall. She couldn't help wondering how much longer it would be before the storm was over and she had to leave.

To a certain extent, her plan to get Frantor used to her presence had worked. He had grown more comfortable with her. He joined her for every meal without argument and had insisted on taking over the cleanup. She frequently joined him in the workroom as work progressed on his fleet of drones. He continued her music lessons, and sang for her occasionally, although not as often as she would have liked.

He even kissed her several more times. Each time the passion flared between them as explosively as it had the first time, but each time something had happened to remind him of his wounds and he had run. The last time had been the previous afternoon when the first of his drones had taken to the air, zooming around the workroom like the large metal insect it resembled. He turned to her with a triumphant cry and pulled her into his arms. Their kiss escalated with its usual speed, and his hand had come up to cover her breast, plucking at her nipple. She had moaned and arched into his hand, and he raised his head.

His lips had been curved with satisfaction until he looked down and saw his metal hand curved around her breast. She watched his mouth tighten before he quickly stepped back. It was during one of the lulls in the storm and he'd actually left the building, rushing out into the snow as she straightened her clothes and swore under her breath.

To her relief, she heard him come back before the storm returned. She'd been pacing around upstairs, trying to decide if she should go after him, when he returned. She'd wanted to go to him, but she knew that he would refuse to talk about it. When he joined her for supper, he didn't mention it and neither did she.

But maybe she was giving him too much space. What would it take to make him stop running? To realize that she wasn't bothered by his prosthetic or by his scars? She hated the fact that he'd been injured, hated the fact that the pain lingered and he still suffered, but it didn't make him any less attractive in her eyes. But how could she convince him that she wanted more?

She sighed and went to check on the compote she was making from some of the fruits stored in the pantry. She dipped her finger into the sauce, then tasted it. Perfect. As she licked her finger to catch the last drops, a thought suddenly occurred to her. It was always the visual reminder of his injuries that stopped him. What if she could encourage him to focus on his other senses instead? She smiled and began to make her preparations.

"I was thinking," she told him as they cleared the table after dinner.

"Yes?"

He sounded cautious, but also intrigued and she hid a smile. He always seemed to like her suggestions, eventually.

"We haven't been making much progress on your cooking lessons."

She'd given him a few basic lessons, but he seemed uncomfortable with them and she wasn't entirely sure why.

"You don't have to teach me," he said quickly.

"I said I would, and I'm a woman of my word." She gave him a cheerful smile as she wiped off the table. "But I think maybe I was going about it the wrong way. Being a good cook isn't just about following a recipe. You have to understand the ingredients. You have to understand how they taste, how they smell and how they go together."

"I suppose that's true."

"So tonight I thought we'd work on that. Sit down, please."

He obeyed, watching warily as she held up the strip of fabric she cut from the bottom of one of his shirts.

"Not being able to see makes your other senses more acute. Will you let me blindfold you?"

She could see the tension in his mouth, but eventually he nodded and held out a hand.

"I will do it."

Her heart ached as she watched him tie the strip of cloth over his mask, running his finger around the edge of his mask to make sure it still concealed his face as he did so frequently.

"I'm ready."

He sounded as if he were about to face the firing squad.

"All right, let's start with something simple. Open your mouth."

Once again, he hesitated, then obeyed. She sprinkled a few grains of salt onto his tongue.

"What's this?"

"Salt, of course."

"Exactly. Now what happens when I add this?"

This time, she dropped a few grains of sugar.

"Sugar," he said immediately.

"That's correct. Can you tell how they react to each other?"

"It's like the sugar makes the salt saltier and vice versa."

"That's right. Let's try a few more things."

He relaxed as she continued, obviously interested, but she had more than just cooking lessons in mind. She sprinkled a tiny amount of hot spice on his tongue.

"That's spicy."

"Yes. And the best way to temper heat is with sweet."

She dipped her finger into some honey, then slid it into his mouth. For a moment, he tensed, but then he wrapped his tongue around her finger and sucked gently. The pull went straight to her aching clit, but she did her best to sound calm and professional.

"You see what I mean?"

He sucked on her finger one more time, then raised his head.

"Still spicy but yes, tempered by the sweetness."

"Excellent. And that concludes the first part of our lesson. You can take off the blindfold now."

"The first part?" he asked as he reached slowly for the strip of cloth.

"Yes." She held out her hand for the blindfold. "Now it's my turn."

"What do you mean?"

"I mean I want you to blindfold me and then let me taste the combinations you come up with. Doesn't that sound… interesting?"

He looked at her and at the blindfold, and then his eyes gleamed from behind the mask.

"Very interesting."

CHAPTER 15

Frantor's fingers threatened to tremble as he carefully tied the blindfold over Florie's eyes. He hadn't realized until that moment how much safer he felt knowing that she couldn't see him, even accidentally. He could look at her as long as he wanted and she wouldn't know that he was staring. He tried so hard during the day not to gaze at her for too long, despite his fascination. He found himself creeping up the stairs each night to watch her as she slept, still awed that such a beautiful, perfect creature should be in his home. That she made it feel like home. The more time he spent with her, the more he found himself foolishly hoping that the storm would never end. That she would stay with him forever.

Her breath was coming faster now as she waited, her luscious pink lips parted and reminding him of the sweet taste of her mouth. He had tried so hard to resist but to have her so close had been an unbearable temptation. Yet every time he had given in to temptation, something had happened which reminded of his deficiencies. But she couldn't see him now and that knowledge gave him courage.

He ran his finger across that plump lower lip, delighting in the way her breath quickened, her chest rising and falling with each breath. She'd taken advantage of his offer and was currently wearing one of his shirts, the neck open to reveal a sliver of pale skin, and he could see her nipples pressing against the thin cloth. Of course he had noticed the signs of her arousal before, but now he could really look, memorizing the way the cloth shifted over those tempting peaks.

"Frantor?" she whispered, her voice shaky.

"I'm right here, sweetheart."

The endearment emerged without conscious thought, his courage bolstered by the knowledge that she couldn't see him.

Those tempting lips curved.

"Aren't you going to feed me anything?"

My cock. The thought flashed across his mind with explosive desire, but he would never betray her trust that way. Instead he dipped his finger into some citrus juice and painted it across her lips. She licked them, then shuddered.

"That's very sour."

"Which means it needs sweetness."

He swirled his finger in the honey and raised it to her lips, but instead of wiping it across them, he slid his finger into her mouth, just as she had done earlier. Her lips immediately closed around his finger, her mouth hot and damp as she sucked on his finger. Fuck, that felt good. Had it affected her the same way when he had done it? Looking back down at those erect nipples, he suspected that it had.

"Does it taste different when you're licking them from my skin?"

"Definitely. Sour and sweet and you."

"Perhaps I should try."

"You should."

He bent down and licked her lips lightly, teasingly.

"Delicious," he agreed. "But I think I need a larger sample."

"It's the only way to be sure," she said breathlessly.

He dipped his finger in the citrus juice again, but this time, instead of painting her lips, he drew his finger from the hollow of her throat down between her breasts. She shivered, her nipples growing even stiffer and the scent of her arousal increasing he followed with the honey. He paused to study his handiwork, mesmerized by the way the golden fluid glistened against her pale skin.

"Aren't you going to taste?" she asked breathlessly.

He started to lower his head, then growled and swept the bowls to one side ignoring the fact that several of them crashed to the ground as he placed her on the table.

"What are you doing?"

"Preparing for my feast."

He lowered his head and licked. Despite the need burning through his veins, he took his time, determined to enjoy every taste from the fragile hollow of her throat to the warmth between her breasts. Her hands came up to clutch at his shoulders, and he started to freeze but remembered the blindfold. He was still safely hidden. He relaxed and nuzzled his head between her breasts before pushing the fabric aside as he worked his way over the soft, full mound until he could stroke his tongue over the taut peak that had tempted him for so long.

A wordless cry escaped her mouth as her back arched, and he smiled. Another quick lick and then he raised his head. Fuck, she was even more beautiful than he had imagined, the distended peak of her nipple still gleaming from his mouth. Impatient with the fabric still blocking his view, he ripped the shirt apart, the buttons scattering across the floor. Her pale skin glowed against the wooden table, her body lush and perfect.

"How do I taste?" she whispered.

"Delicious. But I'm supposed to be trying taste combinations, aren't I?"

The bowl of honey had not been one of the ones to hit the floor and he picked it up now, slowly drizzling it over her nipples and then down over the soft swell of her stomach until he reached the waistband of her pants. He hesitated, looking up at her face. He wished he could see her eyes, but he knew if she'd been looking at him, he would never have had the courage to continue.

"I wish to taste all of you. May I, sweetheart?"

Small white teeth closed over her lower lip, and he was sure that she was going to refuse. But then she nodded.

"Yes, please."

"Are you sure?"

"Yes, but no one has ever..."

"We will go slowly," he promised, as he unfastened her pants and drew them down.

Golden brown curls glistened between her legs, almost unbearably tempting, but she was still biting her lip and he had promised to go slowly. He let the pants fall to the floor, but returned to her honey-covered breasts, even sweeter now. He licked and sucked until every drop of honey was gone and her rosy nipples stood out in stark contrast to her pale skin. She buried her fingers in his hair as he devoted himself to her breasts, but even though she touched the straps of his mask several times, he could ignore them and concentrate on his delightful task.

When her breasts were as clean as he could make them and she was quivering beneath him, he followed the trail of honey down across her stomach, down to the curls concealing her sweet cunt. He gently pushed her legs apart to reveal delicate folds, already flushed and glistening.

He couldn't resist. He leaned forward and took a long, slow lick from her tiny entrance to the small nub peeking out at the top of her slit. Her body quivered, her hands tightening in his hair with a delicious sting.

"Frantor, please."

"I promised you I would go slowly," he murmured, circling his tongue around her swollen clit.

"I don't want slow. I want you to make me come. Now."

He circled her clit again and again, feeling it swell and harden, feeling her muscles tighten. He probed tentatively at her entrance, and her hips immediately arched towards him. *Ah.*

She wanted to be filled. His cock immediately jerked enthusiastically, but his focus was on her pleasure. He pressed his finger into her just as he stroked his tongue directly across her swollen nub. Her hips arched again as she cried out his name, her channel convulsing around him, squeezing his finger in tight, rhythmic pulses and sending him over into his own explosive climax, his body shuddering helplessly against her.

CHAPTER 16

Florie floated in a cloud of hazy pink contentment. Her whole body felt limp and satisfied—and slightly sticky, despite Frantor's best efforts to remove the honey. His head was resting against her thigh, and she ran her fingers slowly through his hair, as thick and soft as she had anticipated. The blindfold had worked as well as she had hoped. She hadn't been sure she would like it, but having her eyes covered had made everything else more sensitive. But now she was impatient to see his face, or at least as much of his face as he permitted. She raised her hand to the strip of fabric, then hesitated.

"Is it all right if I remove the blindfold now?"

He immediately tensed, and then he lifted his head from her thigh. He was no longer touching her, and she suddenly felt very exposed.

"May I?" she repeated.

"Yes."

She could hear the hesitation in that deep, beautiful voice, but she was desperate to see him. As soon as she untied the cloth, she looked for him. To her surprise, he was still standing next to the table, and although his mouth was tense, she could see the hunger in his eyes as he looked down at her. She knew she was blushing as she sat up, her arm automatically rising in an inadequate attempt to cover her breasts.

"You do not need to cover yourself for me. You are beautiful."

She could feel the heat in her cheeks increasing, but she couldn't doubt the sincerity in his voice.

"I'm glad you think so. But can you hand me my shirt?" He obeyed wordlessly, and she looked at the missing buttons and sighed. "I think you ruined your shirt."

"It was worth it."

Still blushing, she pulled the shirt on and held it in place between her breasts.

"As much as I enjoyed that, I think I need to go and wash off the rest of the honey." She hopped down from the table then held out her hand. "Why don't you join me?"

He looked as appalled as if she'd suggested he jump off one of the mountains surrounding the ranch.

"Please? I could even put the blindfold back on if you wanted me to."

"But you might still feel—" He cut off his words and shook his head. "No."

She decided not to press the matter. He had come much further than she had expected. Although as much as she had enjoyed having him touch her, she wanted to touch him as well.

Somehow she suspected that that was going to be an even bigger battle. Still, as long as the snow held out, there was hope.

"All right. I'll go take a bath, all by myself." She was halfway to the bathroom when she turned and gave him a teasing look over her shoulder. "I just hope I don't slip while I'm all alone in there."

"Sweetheart..."

He took a half-step towards her before he stopped and shook his head, his mouth curving.

"I'm sure you will be just fine."

At least he'd relaxed a little with her teasing. She smiled at him again and went to take her bath. As she sat in the swirling waters looking out at the snowy darkness, she thought about what had happened. He'd behaved so differently when she was wearing the blindfold. She hated the fact that his appearance mattered so much to him, and she didn't like the idea of not being able to see him while they were making love. But if that was what it took to make him comfortable...

She climbed out and pulled on one of his clean shirts, not bothering with pants. The shirt reached almost to her knees, and it wasn't as if he hadn't already seen everything. But when she opened the door, the living area was empty. The broken bowls had been cleaned away, as well as all the unbroken bowls, except for the bowl of honey sitting squarely in the middle of the table. She regarded it thoughtfully—had he left it out as a silent request for more? But then why had he returned to the workroom? The strip of fabric they had used as a blindfold was also neatly folded and placed next to the honey.

She didn't really want to wear it to sleep in, but perhaps there was another alternative. Methodically checking each of the windows, she made sure that the heavy curtains covered them completely, including the one next to the bed that she usually left open. Once that was done, she turned off all the lights. The result was much darker than she had expected, even after her eyes adjusted. At least there was still a faint glow coming from the workroom below. She made her way carefully to the head of the stairs.

"I'm going to bed, Frantor. I've closed all the curtains and turned out all the lights."

"Why did you do that?"

"Because it makes it as dark as if we were wearing blindfolds. I thought perhaps you could come and sleep with me."

"I... I don't know."

"Just think about it. We can take this as slowly as you want," she added, echoing his earlier words. "Good night, Frantor."

"Good night, sweetheart."

His response was almost too soft to hear, but she smiled as she made her way across the floor and climbed into the big bed. She waited but there was no sound from below, even after the lights in the workroom went out. She continued to wait but she was almost asleep when the mattress dipped and Frantor joined her.

Her eyes flew open, and she waited breathlessly to see what he would do. He didn't do anything. He was simply lying next to her, his body absolutely still. A minute ticked by, then another, and still he didn't move. This wasn't exactly what she had in mind when she asked him to join her. Perhaps he needed a little more encouragement.

She gave what she hoped sounded like a sleepy sigh and rolled towards him. She ended up pressed against a very large and very warm arm. An arm that was also rigid with tension.

"I know you are not asleep."

His voice sounded stiff, but he hadn't attempted to move away from her so she remained snuggled against his arm—his fully clad arm. At least he was only wearing his shirt—he hadn't brought his cloak to bed as well.

Determined to give it one more attempt, she tried making a soft, ladylike snore. His arm shook and it took her a moment to realize that he was laughing. The knowledge delighted her, even though she would have loved to see his face relaxed and smiling.

"That isn't going to work either."

His voice had relaxed, so she sighed and tucked herself a little closer.

"I give up. No, I'm not asleep." She took a deep breath, breathing in his cool clean scent, then frowned. "How did you know I wasn't asleep?"

"Because I know what you sound like when you're asleep, sweetheart," he murmured in that deep voice.

It wasn't until after he finished speaking that he tensed again—at the same time that the realization hit her.

"How do you know? Have you been up here while I was asleep?"

She had a sudden flashback to that first night when she'd dreamed that he was watching her. What if it hadn't been a dream after all?

"Yes," he said finally.

"But why? We see each other all the time."

"Because I wanted to look at you without worrying…"

"Without worrying that I was watching you back?"

"Yes. I know it was wrong, but I couldn't resist. I'm sorry."

Was she upset? *No*, she decided. She knew him well enough by now to know how vulnerable he felt at the idea of being observed.

"It's all right. I understand. I've been tempted to look at you too." She'd hoped to make him feel better, but his body jerked.

"I haven't," she said quickly. "I would never betray your trust like that."

"I betrayed yours."

"I think we both know it's not the same."

She reached over to pat his chest reassuringly. He grabbed her hand, but it was too late. She had already felt the twisted scars beneath the fabric.

"Oh, Frantor," she cried, her heart breaking.

"I'll leave," he said immediately.

He started to rise but desperate to stop him, she did the only thing she could think of and rolled over on top of him. His whole body froze, as rigid as a statue except for the throbbing pulse of his cock against her stomach.

"Don't leave," she said. "I'm not shocked or horrified, except by the thought of the pain you must have endured."

"I don't need your pity," he growled, but he didn't push her away as he could so easily have done.

"It's not pity. I think you're the bravest, kindest, smartest, sexiest person I've ever met."

She meant every word, and perhaps her sincerity penetrated his defenses as his body loosened, just a little, and his hands came up to rest on either side of her hips.

"Sexiest?"

The disbelief in his voice made her heart ache, but she deliberately kept her own voice light as she rocked back over his cock, suppressing a groan of pleasure.

"That's the one you noticed?"

"I'm not sure I believe any of them," he admitted, "but that one most of all."

"You don't think you're strong? When you can carry a barrel of flour in one arm?"

"Any of my brothers could do so."

"Well I certainly couldn't, and I don't know very many human men who could either. And as for smart, could any of your brothers have created those drones and come up with a plan to protect the ranch?"

"I'm sure Artek or Callum could devise a plan."

"Could they make the drones?"

"Perhaps not," he admitted, and this time he was the one to move her back across his cock.

Her clit was swollen and throbbing, but she forced herself to ignore her arousal. This was more important.

"And as for kind, how many people would allow a strange woman into their home and give up their clothes and their bed and their food just to keep her safe?"

"I'd like to think that most people would."

"So would I, but there are many who would not."

Doing her best to judge the distance in the darkness, and to avoid touching any of his scars, she reached up and pressed her fingers against his mouth.

"And as for sexiest, you gave me the best climax of my life on the kitchen table only a few hours ago."

She felt his lips curve before he spoke.

"Best?"

"Yes," she said sincerely.

So good that she suspected no other man would ever measure up—and she wasn't interested in finding out. Her heart ached at the thought of leaving him.

"I'm glad." His hands tightened on her hips as he began moving her back and forth over the thick ridge of his erection. "But I'm sure I can do better."

CHAPTER 17

Frantor remained awake long after Florie had fallen asleep. She had been correct that making the living area as dark as possible had helped him to relax. But the darkness had its disadvantages as well. He couldn't see her beautiful face or her lush body. He had to rely on her soft cries and the scent of her arousal to guide his attempts to please her —although those attempts had been gratifyingly successful. He had brought her to climax twice more before she fell into an exhausted slumber.

But even in the darkness, he'd been conscious of his scars. She might not be able to see them, but she would still be able to feel them. When she had attempted to snuggle down against his chest, he had moved her to his side instead despite her sleepy protest. Once she was truly asleep, he'd pulled her back into his arms again, holding her tightly long into the night, wishing with all his heart that he could hold her like this every night.

And it was that thought more than any other that had caused him to put her aside, to climb out of their bed and retreat to the workroom. She wouldn't be with him every night, and he couldn't grow used to having her in his arms.

The days that followed felt oddly unreal, stolen moments of time. During the days, he did his best not to touch her—a goal that was rarely successful. Whether they were cooking or making music or working in his workshop, she would tease him or brush against him or simply give him a look from those big green eyes and he would be unable to resist taking her in his arms and kissing her. But in the light of day, he was all too conscious of his scars, and despite the arousal coursing through his veins they did little more than kiss. She never reproached him, even though he suspected that she was just as frustrated.

The nights were different, but they had their limitations as well. He always came to her bed and pleasured her—but he never allowed her to remove his clothes. He had worshiped every inch of her body, but the closest she had come to his was riding his cloth-covered cock, his pants still firmly in place. And he always left before she woke.

The other factor contributing to his sense of stolen time was that the storm was beginning to pass. The clear periods were more frequent and lasted longer. He knew he should make the trip to the ranch house, to see if it was safe for her, but he kept telling himself that the weather was too uncertain. But it had only snowed once that day and he knew he couldn't put it off any longer.

"I think I will check the path to the ranch house tomorrow," he said that night.

She'd just had her first climax of the evening and was lying contentedly in his arms, but her body stiffened at his words.

"And if it's clear?"

"Then it will be safe for you to go to Nelly. To ask her to help you return to your home."

"My home?" She gave a choked laugh. "I thought this—"

His heart skipped a beat, but she didn't continue. Instead, her hand went to his chest, covering his heart in the darkness.

"If this is our last night, I want to feel you. All of you."

"I... I can't. I'm broken, Florie."

"No, you're not," she said fiercely, moving so that she was astride his cock.

Feeling her moving against him, even through the fabric of his pants, always aroused him and he frequently climaxed when she did, but tonight she settled just behind his cock, teasing his shaft through the cloth.

"This part of you isn't broken, is it?" she whispered, sliding those tormenting fingers up and down the thick length.

"I suppose not," he said, "although I suspected it was until I met you."

Her hand tightened as she gave a delighted laugh.

"Then isn't it only fair that I get to experience what I created?" Her hands brushed against him as she carefully unfastened his pants. "Just this one part. Let me at least feel this part of you."

He knew it was a mistake, knew it would only make losing her that much more painful, but with her sweet scent filling his head and her long fingers caressing his aching flesh, he couldn't resist.

"Just my cock," he growled.

"Of course," she agreed as her hand closed around him—or at least tried to close around him. "Oh my goodness."

"What's wrong?" he demanded, already reaching for her hand to pull it away.

"Nothing's wrong," she purred in a low throaty voice. "You feel absolutely perfect." A long, firm stroke of her hand. "So big." Another stroke. "And hard."

"I won't be for much longer if you keep doing that."

He put his hand over hers, but instead of making her stop, he squeezed her hand tighter around his shaft as she stroked him again.

She hummed happily as her thumb came up to stroke across the broad head, collecting the pearls of moisture beading there.

"I want to try something," she whispered as her hand left him, and he had to bite back a protest.

But then she settled back down over him in the position he used so often to bring her to climax, but this time it was entirely different. There were no clothes between them, nothing to prevent him feeling the hot, wet kiss of her cunt directly against his shaft. They both groaned.

"Oh, this is so much better."

She rocked forward as she so often did, his hands automatically going to her hips to assist, but this time he could feel every detail, feel the swollen nub of her clit as it passed over the head of his cock and she gave a choked cry. He gripped her tighter and repeated the movement, determined to wring more of those delightful sounds from her.

"Oh, God—oh, God. Frantor!"

She cried out his name as she climaxed, the liquid heat of her release coating him as he shuddered, on the verge of his own climax. He was so busy trying to control himself that he didn't realize what she was doing when she fumbled between them, but then she adjusted her position and lowered herself over the head of his cock, impossibly tight, impossibly hot, and impossible to resist. He roared and thrust up into her, his body shuddering as his seed erupted in long, helpless jets. For a moment, he lay panting, still shocked at what happened, but he could feel her channel fluttering wildly around him, hear her breath coming in rapid pants, and he was immediately struck with remorse. He knew how small she was—and he was not.

"I—"

"Don't you dare say you're sorry," she said fiercely, even though her voice trembled. "I wanted this. Just give me a minute."

He forced himself to release one of his hands from her hips and ran it down her back in long, soothing strokes until her breathing steadied. Then she deliberately clenched her muscles around him, and they both groaned.

"You're still hard," she whispered.

"You're still touching me."

"Mmm. That's useful."

She rocked back and forth, the familiar motion also completely new and different now that she was impaled on his cock. The small movements were an agonizing pleasure. He wanted more, wanted to thrust into her soft body over and over again, but he forced himself to remain still as she moved, gradually growing bolder. Her hips began to shift restlessly, and he recognized the movement.

Carefully slipping his hand between their bodies, he found the swollen nub of her clit, throbbing against his finger as she quivered and her channel tightened around him again. He knew how tightly she clasped him when she climaxed around his finger, and the thought of her surrounding his cock the same way made him grow impossibly harder. She gasped, her hips moving rapidly and he allowed himself to move in return, thrusting up into her each time she pushed down.

"Oh, God, yes. Just like that," she gasped. Her hands clenched his shoulders, perilously close to the ragged seam where his prosthetic joined his body, but he didn't care. All he cared about was the fiery rush of ecstasy streaking down his spine, about her soft, demanding cries, and about the way she convulsed around him, clasping him as hotly and tightly and perfectly as he had imagined and driving him into a second helpless climax.

CHAPTER 18

A bright light woke Florie, and it took her a moment to realize that it was from sunlight streaming in through a crack where the curtain wasn't flush against the wall. She blinked as her eyes adjusted and saw a flash of blue sky. Her heart sank. It looked as though nothing would stop Frantor from going to the ranch house.

But for right now, he was still here with her. He was asleep, his arm holding her tightly against his side, his breathing deep and regular. Perhaps it wasn't surprising that he was still asleep. She'd climaxed three times around his cock before he finally, reluctantly withdrew and he had accompanied her each time. She'd been afraid that he would leave her, but he had stayed.

Not only stayed, but woken her twice more during the night. Once to feast on her pussy until she was limp and quivering before thrusting into her with deep, hard strokes that sent her reeling from one climax to another. The second time, he was already entering her when she woke. That time, his strokes were slow and thorough, moving so gently that her climax caught her by surprise. He kept whispering her name, his hand stroking her face and her arms, her breasts and her thighs with what felt like loving reverence.

She had wanted so badly to touch him too. To gather him close and whisper that she loved him. But she was afraid to tell him. He kept his wounds so tightly concealed, his heart even more so. She'd hoped for more time. Time to let him accept her feelings, but now time had run out.

She looked up at his face and realized that his mask had come askew, not much, but enough that she could see more of the scar that twisted the corner of his beautiful mouth. He was still asleep—she could push it higher and finally see him for the first time, but she couldn't do that to him. He trusted her, and she would not betray him. His shirt had come open at the neck, but it revealed nothing more than the strong column of his throat, that section of his skin smooth and unscathed. She wanted to slip her hand inside his shirt, to feel his heart beating beneath her hand, but she couldn't do that either. She settled for putting her hand on top of his shirt, still close enough to feel the steady beat of his heart.

His hand came up to cover hers, but not to push her away. Instead, he held it tighter against him as his eyes opened. He smiled down at her, and for one joyous moment she actually thought that everything would be all right. But then his eyes widened behind the askew mask and he pushed her hand away as he practically fell out of bed, fumbling frantically at the mask. His unfastened pants threatened to drop to the ground, and he had to use one hand to yank them up, but not before she saw the twisted mass of scar tissue on his hip. His harsh pants filled the room as he backed away from her like a cornered animal.

"Frantor, it's all right. You're safe with me. Do you understand? You're safe." She was afraid to go to him, afraid to trigger more panic, but she held out her hand. "You're safe. Come back to me."

His breath stuttered, and she prayed that she was reaching him, but then there was a harsh knock on the workroom door, followed immediately by a stern male voice calling his name. He whirled around, and as he did the mask slipped free, falling to the ground, the plaster shattering as it hit. For the first time, she saw his full face. A terrible scar stretched from his hairline down across his right eye to the corner of his mouth, a twisted strip of darker flesh from a wound that must have barely avoided blinding him in that eye.

"Oh no," she gasped, pressing her hands against her aching chest. How he must have suffered.

She tried to rise, to go to him, but as soon as she spoke he gave a horrible cry, like that of a wounded animal, and then he was gone, flinging himself down the stairs.

"No, Frantor. Wait!" she cried as she scrambled to her feet, tripping over the sheet as she tried to pull it around herself.

An older alien with a stern face appeared at the top of the stairs. She recognized the purple skin and towering dark horns as belonging to the male who usually accompanied Nelly's husband into town, but his identity didn't matter.

"What did you do to Frantor? Where did he go?"

She hurried towards the stairs, the sheet still threatening to trip her with every step, but he showed no signs of moving aside.

"He left," the male said in a deep, calm voice. "Are you all right?"

"What do you mean he left? He went out in the snow?" Her heart skipped a beat. "But he's not dressed for it. He doesn't have his boots or his c-cloak."

Her voice stuttered over the last word as tears began to gather in her eyes. For the first time, the purple male looked alarmed, taking a slight step back.

"Do not be concerned. Artek went after him."

"Of course I'm concerned," she snapped. "He was so scared, and he didn't understand. I have to go after him."

"You cannot go after him wrapped in a sheet. It will not help either of you if you die from exposure."

"Fine. I'll get dressed first, but then I'm going after him. This is all my fault."

"Why don't you get dressed and then you can tell me why you believe it to be your fault?" For the first time, a hint of a smile crossed that stern face. "I do not believe that my mate would appreciate me being in the same room with a female in your present lack of attire."

"I'll be happy to tell her that I have absolutely no interest in you," she snapped impatiently, but he was right. She had to get dressed in order to go after Frantor. She was halfway to the bathroom to get dressed when she realized what he had said and shot a glance back over her shoulder.

"What do you mean, your mate? Didn't Nelly marry Commander Artek?"

"Indeed. I have the honor of being wedded to Pearl."

"Pearl Bennett?"

She wasn't close friends with the other woman, but she'd always had the impression that the attractive widow was not remotely interested in marrying a second time. Then again, would anyone have expected her to have fallen in love with a wounded, prickly, masked alien? Frantor! Her brief curiosity about Pearl's marriage disappeared as she hurried to get dressed.

"Now," she demanded as soon as she returned. "Take me to Frantor."

"I cannot." He held up a hand before she could protest. "Artek went after him, but I do not know where either of them are and it could be a good distance away. We move more quickly than humans."

She huffed an exasperated breath, but she suspected he was right.

"Fine. Then I'll just wait right here until he comes back."

He hesitated for a moment. "May I make an alternate suggestion?"

"You can, but I already suspect that I'm not going to like it."

"I was going to suggest that you accompany me to the ranch house. A number of things have happened since you arrived here."

She crossed her arms and glared at him.

"So?"

"You are not the only human female who was taken," he said calmly.

"I wasn't?"

She recalled Frantor telling her about the story Nelly had told them.

"How many others are there?"

"Five, including yourself. Plus Nelly and my Pearl, of course."

"Did you abduct her too?"

His face hardened. "I did not, just as Frantor did not take you."

"Great. Some alien Santa decided to go around gifting women to all of you."

She sighed and strode over to the window, pulling the curtain all the way open now that the damage had been done. The sky above was a brilliant blue, the sun sparkling down on the thick layer of snow that stretched down the valley and covered the mountains rising on either side. The sight was beautiful enough to take her breath away, but all she could think about was that Frantor was somewhere out there, alone in the snow.

"I need to be here for him when he comes back." He would come back, wouldn't he?

"I understand why you feel that way," the purple male said as he joined her at the window, making her jump. He moved as silently as Frantor. "But he appears to be... distraught."

Another wave of guilt washed over her.

"When one is injured, one tends to seek safety. This mill has been his safe place."

Her throat threatened to close.

"You mean now it's not because I... I'm here?"

"That is not what I'm saying. I am simply suggesting that it might be best to give him space to heal."

To heal from the damage I caused. Her heart wanted her to stay, but maybe he was right. Maybe Frantor did need time to calm down.

"Fine."

"I am now acquainted enough with human females to understand that that word does not actually signify agreement."

"Well it's the only one you're going to get. What's your name, anyway?"

"I am Callum."

She stalked towards the stairs, refusing to even look around. Her instincts were screaming at her to stay, but she didn't want to risk hurting Frantor any further.

"Take me to meet the rest of these kidnapped brides."

CHAPTER 19

Frantor pushed past Artek and fled, unaware of anything except the need to run, to hide. The icy cold of the snow burned against his bare feet, and the legs of his pants were soon wet and freezing, sending streaks of pain along the nerves damaged by his injuries, but those pains were nothing to the ache in his heart. His initial panic began to fade, replaced by the pain of her rejection.

Florie's horrified face danced in front of his eyes. How could he have been so careless as to reveal himself to her? And how could he have been so foolish to believe there was even a chance that such a beautiful, perfect female would care for him? He had deluded himself into believing that her soft touches came from more than just a desire to comfort him.

He stumbled over a rock and came to a halt, his breath coming in harsh, gulping pants as he realized he was on the bank of the river. Despite the lengthy storm, the water had not frozen, although chunks of ice tumbled past in the rapid current. The water looked cold and pitiless, but it promised oblivion. For one dreadful second, he actually considered throwing himself into the raging current, but once again Florie's face appeared in his mind. Not horrified this time, but soft and smiling at him.

No matter how shocked she had been by his appearance, he knew she would feel sorrow at his loss and he couldn't do that to her. He couldn't cause her any more pain.

"What the hell do you think you're doing?" Artek's hand closed on his arm and snatched him away from the edge of the river. "You could have fallen in."

He'd never seen his brother look quite so angry, his usual control shattered, and it reminded him that Florie was not the only one who would mourn his loss.

"Don't worry. I wasn't planning on jumping in."

"Good," Artek snapped, before wrestling himself back under control.

He looked past him, half-hoping, half-dreading to see Florie following in Artek's footsteps, but there was no beautiful female making her way across the snow.

"Where's Florie? You didn't leave her alone, did you?"

"Callum is with her."

Despite his relief that she was not alone and unprotected, a growl threatened to emerge from his throat. He didn't like the idea of her being alone with another male, especially not one with Callum's calm, commanding presence and unscarred face.

"Why are you here?"

"I came after you. Here."

Artek thrust his cloak and boots at him. He considered refusing them, but decided it would be a foolish gesture. The warmth of the boots made his feet burn even more, although he knew it would pass. He pulled the cloak around his shoulders, no longer worried about concealment, but grateful for the warmth.

"I meant why did you come to the mill?"

"We came to check on you. Both of you."

Artek turned and started to walk back towards the mill, and he reluctantly followed him. Now that his first panic had subsided, he was aware that it would be foolish to remain outside in the snow.

"You knew Florie was here? How?"

"Benjar, of course. When he and Endark went to gather their brides, he decided that both you and Gilmat needed wives as well."

"Gilmat?"

Even after all their time together, the huge, quiet male remained a mystery. He knew the other male had a vast intelligence and an ingrained sense of loyalty, but he guarded his feelings even more closely than Frantor. He suspected that Endark was the only one who truly understood him.

But although he was surprised that Gilmat had been included, he was not surprised that his impetuous youngest brother had been behind the scheme.

"I thought perhaps it was Benjar who left her with me."

"Indeed. And it was not the only mischief that he and Endark caused. An avalanche has blocked the pass through the mountains to Wainwright, and I expect it will remain blocked long after the thaws set in."

That means Florie can't leave me. The sudden wave of hope made him almost dizzy, but then he shook his head. The length of time made no difference. The horror on her face had made her feelings clear.

"Perhaps Callum and Florie will become better acquainted," he said stiffly. The older male had never shown any signs of interest in a female, but how could any male resist his Florie?

"I suspect his bride would not be happy with that," Artek said dryly.

"You mean that Callum also kidnapped a bride?"

He couldn't imagine a less likely scenario for the rigidly correct older male.

"No, he found her when she came after Benjar's bride." Artek shook his head. "It's a long story, and I'll tell you all about it later. But there is a more important matter to discuss first. There is a possibility that we may come under attack."

"And you left Florie alone?" he snarled, increasing his pace.

"I left her with Callum, and he's going to take her back to the ranch house. Not that there is any reason to suspect an immediate threat," Artek added calmly. "But we need to be prepared."

"Why? What happened?"

Artek sighed. "It sems the former owner of this ranch sent for a bride many years ago, but she never made it. Her ship crashed and she was injured, but she was nursed back to health by a pack of Vultor."

Vultor? He knew little about them except they had a reputation for savagery and the ability to shift into a stronger, alternate form. Nursing a stranger back to health did not sound like their typical behavior.

"Why did they do that?"

"I don't know. She was female, and they might simply have felt sorry for her. We know very little about them other than the tales the humans tell, and they appear to be somewhat biased."

"If they nursed her back to health, why didn't she marry Josiah?"

"Apparently, she fell in love with the alpha of the Vultor pack. They came to tell Josiah and he promised to leave the ranch to her after his death as long as they left the area."

"But this is our ranch," he protested. In spite of everything that had happened, he did not want to leave it.

"Yes. She died in childbirth and the child with her."

"Then I don't understand the problem."

"The pack leader went mad without her."

Artek shot him a quick glance and he nodded, remembering the way he'd felt standing at the edge of the river. At least his love was still alive, even if she wasn't with him. His love. The words brought him to a halt as he finally admitted what he tried so hard to deny. He'd been in love with her since the first moment she reached across the table and took his hand.

How am I going to live without her?

Artek had stopped as well, waiting patiently as he finally acknowledged the truth.

"I understand how that could have happened," he said at last.

"I thought you might." Artek resumed walking and he followed him. "The Alpha sired another child and passed along his madness. That male is dead now, thanks to Endark, but another member of the tribe warned him that his followers might decide to pursue vengeance. I do not know how serious the threat is," Artek added as the mill came into sight, "but we need to be prepared." He looked up at the surrounding mountains and shook his head. "I do not see any way to safeguard every possible path into the valley."

"I may be able to help with that," he said as he reached for the door handle. His hand was shaking. Would Florie still be here? Or would she have seized the opportunity to leave with Callum?

As soon as he entered, he knew that she had gone. Only the lingering hint of her sweet scent remained. His chest felt as if it cracked open, as raw and aching as when he'd first been injured. The icy depths of the river called to him once more, but nothing had changed. Not only could he not hurt her that way, he was needed. He had to protect her, protect all of them.

He walked over to the worktable and the neat rows of drones he had created—that *they* had created.

"I think these will help."

His voice sounded odd, hollow and empty, and Artek put his hand on his shoulder as he came to join him.

"Drones?"

"Yes. I've been working on a pattern that should enable them to cover the entire valley. It won't be perfect—a single individual could certainly slip through—but they should be able to detect any type of concentrated attack." He reached for his datapad, his voice still empty. "We should review the possible patterns."

"I agree." Artek hesitated. "Perhaps it would be best to go back to the main house so that the others—"

"No!"

She had chosen to leave him. He couldn't stand the thought of facing her again, knowing that she did not want him. Especially now that his worst fears had come true. All of his brothers were happily mated, and he was alone. He would always be alone.

CHAPTER 20

Florie followed Callum as he headed back along the river. He was clearing a path for her, carefully stamping down the snow to make it easier for her to walk, but that didn't stop her from glaring at his back. She still didn't think she was doing the right thing by leaving the mill. Several times she almost turned around and went back, but the same thought stopped her every time. What if Frantor didn't want her there? What if her presence would only add to the pain she caused him?

She was so busy debating with herself that she almost ran into Callum when he stopped at the end of a small incline. Startled, she looked up and saw the ranch house, an impressive-looking building with two long wings on either side of a sharply angled center section. The fact that it was so close was oddly reassuring. Frantor could easily have reached it during one of the many lulls in the weather, and yet he had stayed with her.

At least until I chased him away. Her throat threatened to close as she followed Callum across a small courtyard towards the entry doors. Before they reached them, one of the doors flew open and Nelly came flying out.

"Florie! I'm so glad to see you. But where's Frantor? Is he all right?"

She burst into tears

Nelly gave her a dismayed look, then put her arm around Florie's shoulder and glared at Callum.

"What did you do to her?"

"I didn't do anything."

"Then why is she crying, and why isn't Frantor here?"

Without waiting for a response, Nelly urged Florie inside and across the huge vaulted living room with a magnificent view out over the valley.

"Come on. We'll go to Artek's office and have a nice, quiet chat."

She hurried Florie past the kitchen just as a burst of laughter erupted, and Florie had to fight down the urge to march in and tell them that they were all being insensitive jerks. Didn't they know that her heart was breaking and Frantor was out in the snow, alone and barefoot?

Nelly led her into a comfortable office with another stunning view and walls lined with bookshelves.

"Now tell me what happened," Nelly said, urging her down onto a small couch and sitting next to her.

"Frantor's mask came off and he has this terrible scar and I was upset that he'd been injured so badly, but he didn't understand

and thought I was scared of him and he ran away into the snow and he doesn't even have his boots!" she wailed.

"Shush," Nelly said, taking her hand in a comforting grip. "I'm sure everything is going to be fine. I'm just trying to understand. Did you say that Frantor was wearing a mask? I don't remember that."

"You saw him?" she demanded. Why would he have revealed himself to Nelly after being so determined to remain hidden from her?

Nelly shook her head. "Not really. He saved my life, did you know that?"

"No."

"He was very kind to me when I came. He helped me understand the way things were, but I never saw him and I could never get him to come into the house."

"He said you left him cookies."

"I did, and he always took them. But then he stopped and I was worried, so I decided to go to the mill. On the way, I was attacked by an adyani."

She shivered, and Florie echoed her. The adyani were one of the few natural predators on Cresca. They were rarely seen by humans, but they were known for their vicious attacks.

"Frantor heard me scream and came to my rescue," Nelly continued. "He even brought me back here and called for Drakkar."

"So you did see him."

"No, I fell when I was trying to get away from the adyani and hit my head. I only caught a glimpse of his face before I lost consciousness, but I'm sure he wasn't wearing a mask."

"He probably wasn't. He made it after someone kidnapped me and left me with him."

Nelly sighed. "Believe it or not, Benjar's intentions were good. He thought Frantor needed someone to keep him company. And I have to say I agree with him."

"I do too, and I want to be that person. I love him, Nelly, but he ran away from me."

"I ran away from Artek too, but it wasn't because I didn't love him. You need to talk to him."

"That's what I wanted to do, but Callum said that I should give him some time to calm down."

Nelly huffed. "That sounds like something a male would say. The longer they have to brood, the more wrongheaded they get."

"So I should go back?" she asked eagerly.

Nelly bit her lip. "I must admit, in this case I'm not sure. And there are some other things going on right now that complicate matters."

"Like what?"

"Well, for one thing, the pass is closed. There was an avalanche after they brought you through the pass. An intentional avalanche. And now the pass is blocked and probably will be until summer."

Summer?

"My diner," she whispered.

"I know. I'm sorry. I know how much it means to you."

It did, and yet at the moment it seemed so far away. She gave Nelly a rueful look.

"It's not the end of the world. I own the building so it's not like anyone can kick me out, and I have enough savings that I could reopen it."

"Could?" Nelly's eyes sparkled mischievously, and she gave her a shaky smile in return.

"I suppose it would depend on what happens here. I can't imagine Frantor living in town." She sighed. "But I can't imagine not working."

"You don't have to worry about that." Nelly grinned at her. "Pearl and I have been working on ways to generate income for the ranch, and I'm sure you'll have lots of good ideas as well."

"I might," she said, thinking of the bounty in Frantor's pantry, then sighed. "But that's not really what's important. What's important is talking to Frantor."

"You know, Drakkar ran away from Kitty as well, even though he said he was doing it for her sake," Nelly said thoughtfully. "I think we should go and talk to her."

"Kitty? You mean the girl who just had the baby?" Out of wedlock, which had been a huge scandal in Wainwright, but the girl had held her head high and refused to name the father. "Who else is here?"

"Pearl, of course, and her sister Ruby. Ruby is with Benjar. And then there's Becky and her brother—she's with Endark. And Julie is with Gilmat."

"Julie Watson? Her mother must be having a fit." The overbearing matron was one of her least favorite people, but the girl had always seemed nice enough.

Nelly laughed. "I'm sure she is, and I'm equally sure that there will be hell to pay when the pass finally opens, but trust me, Gilmat can handle her. Now let's go find Kitty."

Florie followed her back down the passageway, but decided not to go into the kitchen. The last thing she wanted was to be sociable when she was still feeling so uncertain about her future. Through the open door, she caught a glimpse of a huge green male. All of the brothers were large, but he was the biggest male she had ever seen, his skin a rich deep green, the strands of his hair waving gently as if a breeze caressed them even inside the house. He adjusted his position, and she saw Julie perched on his knee, the pretty blonde looking tiny next to him—and were those vines curled around her arm?

Before she could decide, Nelly came back, accompanied by a strange male. Another big alien with glittering coppery skin, short dark horns, and massive wings—*wings!*—that flared behind him as he walked. He gave her a cool, assessing glance, his expression forbidding.

"Kitty was nursing the baby," Nelly said breathlessly. "But I brought Drakkar instead. He's our doctor."

"I know, Frantor mentioned him."

His face hardened even more.

"Not favorably, I'm sure."

"Actually, he spoke very highly of you."

"There is no reason why he should. I failed him."

"You did not," Nelly said immediately. "Artek said you saved his life."

"But I could not heal him. Now he will not even let me try."

"Try? You mean you could help him?" she asked eagerly.

"Why? Are his scars so appalling?"

His voice was ice cold, and she glared at him.

"I don't give a fuck about his scars, but he does. That's why he hides away from everyone."

Drakkar returned her glare, then sighed, his face relaxing.

"I know. And honestly I cannot remove them. But he is in constant discomfort and that I could help with." He studied her again, his face softer this time. "Do you love him?"

"Yes." Her throat threatened to close again. "Very much."

"Then why are you here without him?"

"He ran away because I was upset when I saw his scars. He thought I was going to reject him. I wanted to wait and talk to him, but Callum said to give him time to settle down."

"Callum was wrong," Drakkar said. "Frantor has been alone since he was injured. He does not need more time by himself. He needs to know that he is loved."

"Then I'm going back, right now."

"You can't go by yourself," Nelly said. "That's one of the other problems I mentioned."

"I will accompany you," Drakkar said, then raised an eyebrow at Nelly. "Unless you do not think that I will be sufficient protection?"

Nelly laughed. "I can't imagine that Florie would be safer with anyone else. Except Artek, of course," she added loyally.

"Of course." Drakkar's voice actually sounded sincere before he turned to Florie. "Are you ready?"

"Yes. Let's go right now."

She gave Nelly a quick hug and a whispered thanks, then followed Drakkar back through the living room and outside. Since the path had already been broken, he remained courteously at her side.

"Do you really think you could help his pain?" she blurted out as they started down the hill.

"To a certain extent. Some of his muscles are irreparably damaged."

"It seems to help when I massage them. Should I keep doing that?"

"He let you do that?"

"Reluctantly, at least at first."

"He refused to let me try."

"I have ways of persuading him that you don't."

He smiled for the first time, the expression transforming his rather hard face. *He really is quite attractive*, she thought dispassionately, but all she wanted was the stubborn wounded male who had run from her. *He's not going to run from me again*, she swore. Even if she had to cling to him like one of those vines that had been wrapped around Julie's arm. She just prayed that he would listen to her and forgive her.

"There is one thing you should know," Drakkar said. "Sometimes a male rejects a female because he cares too much. Because he thinks it's in her best interest."

"Is that what you did?" she asked, remembering what Nelly had said.

He shrugged a shoulder, a wing fluttering behind him, but he didn't respond.

"Don't worry. I won't let him do that to me." *I hope.*

They were next to the river now and her pulse started to speed up. Was he back at the mill already? Even if he weren't, she would wait for as long as it took. And she wouldn't leave until he listened to her.

They came around a curve at the riverbank, and there was Frantor.

Frantor, walking towards them. His hood was back, his face uncovered, and she had never been so glad to see anyone in her entire life. She forgot about being patient, about giving him time and understanding, and she ran towards him, determined to get to him before he could leave her again. But he didn't run away. He closed the distance between them with a few rapid strides, and she flung herself into his arms, laughing and crying as she kissed every inch of his face that she could reach.

"I'm so sorry. I was just surprised. I love you, Frantor."

He shuddered, and dropped to his knees, still holding her.

"I love you too. Don't ever leave me again."

"Never," she promised and kissed him.

CHAPTER 21

She loves me.

The knowledge sang through Frantor's veins as he pulled Florie close, her soft curves fitting so perfectly against him, making him whole. She stopped kissing him long enough to pull back and look up at his face. The impulse to flinch away was still there, but the fact that she loved him gave him the courage to remain steady as she studied him. Her hand came up to lightly trace the edge of his scar.

"I wasn't horrified," she whispered. "It just hurts to know how much you have suffered."

"It does," Drakkar said quietly.

He had seen the other male accompanying Florie, but his attention had been on her. He'd almost forgotten that Drakkar was there.

"I know you did everything you could."

He had said the words before, he had even meant them, but with Florie in his arms there was no hesitation in his voice, and this time Drakkar seemed to accept them. He dipped his head.

"Since it appears that you are not going to repeat my foolish mistake, I am returning to my mate. See me when you're ready and we will discuss options."

With the flutter of wings, he was gone.

"Drakkar has a mate?"

"What did he mean, options?" They both spoke at the same time, and she laughed, immediately followed by a shiver.

"It's too cold for you out here," he said immediately. "Do you want to go back to the ranch house?"

"No, I want to go home. To our house."

Our house. He liked the sound of those words, and he smiled as he rose with her in his arms and started back down the river towards the mill.

"I'm sorry I left. I didn't want to, but Callum convinced me that you needed some time."

"You're the only one I need," he said, then sighed. "But perhaps he was right as well. He gave Artek a chance to talk some sense into me."

"What did he say?"

"He reminded me that the ones we love are always worth fighting for."

Of course it hadn't been quite as straightforward as that, but he knew it would distress her to know how alone and rejected he had felt. He had tried to concentrate as Artek discussed various options for using the drones to monitor the valley, but it was no use. Artek finally stopped in mid-sentence and studied his face.

"Why did you try and disable that missile site alone?"

What? Why was Artek digging up the past now?

"You know why," he said impatiently. "Because they were about to strike and I couldn't stand the thought of another village being destroyed, of more families being lost."

There hadn't been time to wait for the others to catch up with him. He had known he probably wouldn't make it out alive, but he hadn't had a choice.

"You fought for what you believed in," Artek said. "You were willing to take on an enemy site on your own because of those beliefs."

He shrugged uncomfortably and looked away.

"Like I said, I didn't think I had a choice."

"And now you have a choice?"

"I don't understand. "

"Do you love her?"

The realization was too raw, too close to the surface, but he couldn't deny it.

"Yes."

"Then I'll ask you again, is there any choice other than to fight for her? For her love?"

His fingers tightened on the edge of the worktable, fear and certainty fighting for dominance—an unexpectedly familiar feeling.

"I'm afraid," he admitted.

"You were afraid when you attacked the enemy as well."

Artek was right, and yet somehow this terrified him even more.

"Do you really believe that she doesn't return your feelings?" Artek asked,

He thought back over the time they'd spent together. Of the way she worked with him and cooked for him and talked to him, and the look on her face when she listened to him sing. He thought of the way that she teased him and touched him, and he thought about the blindfold she had prepared, just to make him comfortable. A little spark of hope began to grow inside of him. Was it possible after all? And if she had accepted everything else about him, perhaps she could eventually accept his scars as well.

"I think perhaps she does."

"Then that is worth fighting for."

Yes. He hesitated for a moment longer, looking over at the cabinet which contained the supplies he'd used to make his mask. Should he make another one? *No*, he decided. He would if she asked him to, but it was time to reveal himself completely.

Artek nodded.

"I'll take these schematics back to the house and discuss them with Callum. Now go."

He never obeyed an order more readily. He'd been prepared to face his brothers and their unknown human mates if necessary, but instead she had been returning to him. Gratitude filled him as he tightened his arms around her and she smiled up at him.

"Are you sure I'm not too heavy?"

"I could carry you all day," he assured her, but the mill was only a short distance away. He carried her upstairs, then placed her on her feet. She gave him an expectant look, but he left her there, left her long enough to cross to the windows and pull all the curtains wide open, letting sunlight flood the room.

"You don't have to do this," she said softly.

"I think I do."

But despite his certainty, his hands threatened to shake as he returned to her and removed first her cloak and then his own. They shook again as he began to unfasten his shirt, and she put her hand over his.

"You don't have to do this right now. You can take your time."

"I know, sweetheart. But I know I'm safe with you."

Her eyes filled with tears.

"You are safe with me, but that doesn't mean that I'm not going to react. I might be angry or sad or upset. But those feelings are *for* you, not because of you. I love you, and that's not going to change."

He nodded, unable to speak, and she took a step back, waiting patiently as he continued unfastening his shirt. Her face paled as he took a deep breath and pushed the shirt off his shoulders, revealing the ragged seam where his prosthetic was attached and the twisted scars that covered the left side of his body. But she didn't flinch, or run, just stood there watching as he toed off his boots and let his pants drop. The scar tissue continued down past his hip onto his thigh, but she had already touched those scars when she had massaged his leg. At the memory of her hands touching him, his cock began to stiffen, and her eyes widened, lingering there for a moment before looking back up at his face.

"Thank you for being so brave, and thank you for trusting me."

"You are not repulsed?"

"Not at all."

She closed the distance between them, her soft curves nestling against him.

"I care about what's in here." She gently touched his head. "And in here."

She placed her hand over his heart and he covered it with his own just as he had done when he first woke. They stood together in silence for a long moment, and then her smile turned teasing.

"And perhaps, just a little, I care about this."

Her long fingers curved around his cock and tugged gently.

"You're wearing too many clothes," he growled.

"I can take care of that."

He reached for her but she danced back, shaking her head playfully.

"Now it's your turn to watch."

She deliberately echoed his movements, slowly unfastening the shirt she was wearing and letting it slip free before kicking off her boots and pushing her pants down over her luscious hips. Then she walked back into his arms, not flinching as her soft skin came into contact with his many scars. Her hand came up to his face, brushing his hair back, and she smiled.

"I much prefer seeing your face rather than seeing that mask."

"And I much prefer having you naked in my arms."

The direct contact of skin against skin felt so good. How had he lived without it for so long?

"I could just rub you all over me," he murmured.

"I think some parts rub against each other more satisfactorily than other parts."

He laughed, picking her up and carrying her to the bed. "Then I think we need to find out exactly which parts those are."

CHAPTER 22

Florie pressed herself closer to Frantor, relishing the feel of his skin against hers. She could feel the difference in texture between his scarred skin and his undamaged skin, and her heart ached at what had happened to him. She had suspected it was bad, but she hadn't understood the full extent of his injuries until now. They made no difference in how she felt about him, and she was determined to prove it to him. Once they were in bed, she pulled back a little, and he gave her a puzzled look.

"I'm not going anywhere," she said. "I just want to look and admire."

"Admire?" he asked, clearly skeptical and, she suspected, still not entirely comfortable with her looking at him.

"Yes, admire. Do I need to tell you all the things I like about you?"

"I know there is one part that you like," he said, and she grinned at him.

"You're right. I do like that part very much. But it's not the only one."

"Such as?"

"I love your hair and the way it falls over your brow—and the way it feels when I'm holding onto it while you lick me." She saw his cock jerk out of the corner of her eye, but she continued to concentrate on his face. "I love how expressive your eyes are. Even behind the mask they helped me to understand what you were feeling. And of course I love your mouth—it's exceptionally talented."

His body had relaxed and once again he tried to reach for her, but she shook her head.

"I love how broad your shoulders are and how strong. And all these sexy muscles."

She trailed her hand across his chest, deliberately including both his scarred and non-scarred areas as she moved lower. Her fingers skated lightly across his cock, delighting in the way it rose to meet her before she moved on to his thighs. She didn't get very far before he groaned and sat up.

"You're killing me, sweetheart."

He swung his feet over the edge of the bed, pulling her onto his lap. his cock throbbed between them, a tantalizing promise pressed against her and a wave of desire swept over her. She wiggled impatiently, trying to lift her hips and take him inside, but he easily held her in place.

"I thought you weren't in a hurry. Did you run out of things you admired?"

"No, but I thought I'd save the rest for another time."

"Then I guess that means it's my turn. I haven't told you all the things I admire about your body."

"You don't have to," she said quickly. "I believe you."

"But I want to. For example, I love your hair."

"And my eyes and my mouth?" she teased.

"Yes," he said thoughtfully. "But perhaps not for the same reasons. For example, I love using your hair to guide you."

He wrapped his hand in her hair and tugged it, not hard enough to hurt, but hard enough to send an unexpected streak of excitement to her clit.

"And your mouth is equally talented."

She tried to lean forward and kiss him, but he held her in place.

"And of course there are these amazingly luscious breasts."

He cupped one, testing the heavy weight against his hand before reaching up and plucking at her nipple, the firm pressure adding to her arousal. Despite his attempt at a casual tone she knew he was equally excited. His cock jerked every time he touched her, seeming to grow harder each time she managed to rock her hips forward enough that her clit was directly against the thick shaft. He wasn't even moving, and she was already on the verge of coming.

"Frantor, please."

"What is it, sweetheart?"

He tried to sound innocent, but she could hear the betraying gruffness in his voice. Good. At least she wasn't the only one suffering.

"I need you," she said, trying to wiggle closer.

He cupped her face with his hand. "I need you too."

"Then take me."

He groaned, then started to lift her hips. She quivered with anticipation, but instead of lifting her onto his cock, he slid her back down his shaft, rubbing her swollen clit directly against the thick, veined surface. She shivered again and he repeated the movement, making sure she felt the slow drag of the long descent.

Her breath caught as he lifted her higher, once again teasing her entrance before sliding her back down his shaft. She could have groaned with frustration, even though her body was hovering on the edge of climax. She couldn't wait any longer. When he raised her the next time, holding her tantalizingly over his cock, she leaned forward and lightly nipped his chest. He jerked and his grip loosened for just a moment, just long enough for her to slam herself down over his cock.

Oh, God. As ready as she was, she was still swollen from the previous night, and he seemed even larger in this position. She panted, willing her body to adjust, and then he rocked against her, just a fraction, but enough to transform the overwhelming stretch into an incredible fullness.

"Is this one of the parts you admire?" she asked breathlessly.

"This perfect cunt? Absolutely."

He started to lift her hips again, and she didn't protest, content to be impaled on his massive cock. But then he released her, letting her slide down hard and fast, and her climax roared through her in a never-ending wave.

"Perfect," he repeated, and then he began to thrust.

"What options?" she asked, a long time later.

Their bodies were still pressed together, and he was running his hand lovingly over her skin.

"I don't understand."

"Earlier. Drakkar said to come see him to discuss options."

His muscles tensed briefly, but then he sighed and the tension drained away.

"He thinks I should get a new prosthetic. But this one works perfectly well."

She looked skeptically at the clearly inflamed skin where the arm was connected to his body. "It doesn't look very comfortable."

"It's functional. That's all that matters."

"But if Drakkar thinks you should replace it, I'm sure he has a good reason."

His lips pressed together in a stubborn line.

"He doesn't think that the graft was completely successful, that a new one would be better adapted to my body."

"Which sounds perfectly reasonable. Why don't you want to do it?"

His lips were still pressed together, and for a moment she thought he wouldn't answer her, but finally he sighed again.

"I would have to leave the ranch and go to the medical facility in Port Cantor. Everyone would stare at me. But it's more than that. I hate hospitals. In my mind, they are places of pain and suffering and death. I don't want to go back to one. Unless... does this bother you?"

He brushed his hand across the ragged flesh, and she shook her head.

"If you mean does the sight bother me, no. What bothers me is that it is painful for you."

"I'm used to it."

Her heart ached. "But you shouldn't have to be. It's your decision, and I'll support whatever you decide. If you do decide to have it replaced, I'll go with you."

He gave her a thoughtful look.

"Would you rather live somewhere like Port Cantor? A large city where you would have access to anything you wanted?"

"Not at all. I chose Wainwright specifically because it was small and peaceful."

"And it is where your business is located. Do you want us to move there once the pass is clear?"

"You would do that for me?"

He cupped her face. "I would do anything to make you happy."

She believed him, but she also knew how unhappy he would be living in Wainwright. And while there were many good people in town, they did not handle strangers well, especially not alien strangers.

"I've been thinking about that, actually. Nelly mentioned that they're looking for opportunities to profit from the products on the ranch. I thought perhaps my assistants Susan and Roger could continue to run it as a restaurant, but on a smaller scale. Then we could also use it as a store, to sell not only the things that we can produce, but other products from the town or the outlying farms. I might have to go there a few times to get things set up, but we wouldn't need to live there."

He gave a huge sigh of relief. Then he bent his head and kissed her and there was no more discussion about living arrangements.

The sun was beginning to sink into the trees when she finally sat up and stretched.

"I guess I should think about what to have for dinner."

"I have a suggestion," he said slowly. "What if we join the others at the ranch house?"

"I know Nelly would love that, but are you sure?"

"Yes, I think I am. I don't want you to live in isolation here, but I don't want to be separated from you either."

"You don't have to do this because of me."

"It's not just because of you. I had withdrawn from my brothers as well. Seeing Artek, even under these unfortunate circumstances earlier, reminded me that I've missed them."

"In that case, I'd be delighted to go with you to the house."

She washed quickly, then pulled on the dress she had worn when she arrived. His eyes heated when she joined him again, and she immediately decided to talk to Nelly about obtaining some more clothes. His clothes were comfortable enough, but she liked seeing that look of appreciation on his face.

Hand in hand, they walked back along the snowy path towards the house. The lights were already on inside against the gathering dusk, and they could hear laughter.

"Are you sure you want to do this?" she asked again when he stopped to look at the house.

"I'm sure. I spent a lot of time out here alone, watching and listening. I didn't feel as if I belonged in there, especially after Nelly came, but I don't feel that way anymore. I belong with you, and that's what matters. But because I belong with you, I also feel as if I belong inside. Does that make sense?"

"It makes perfect sense. I never found the place where I fit, until now."

She took his hand and they walked inside. A startling number of people seemed to be gathered around the fireplace, but Nelly was the first to see them.

"Oh my God. You came. You finally came."

She flung herself at Frantor, and burst into tears. He patted her back awkwardly, giving Florie a helpless look over her head. Before she could step in and rescue him, Artek gently tugged Nelly away from Frantor and into his own arms.

"She's a little overemotional now because of the pregnancy," he said.

Pregnant? Florie's knees suddenly threatened to give out. She had assumed that choosing Frantor meant giving up the possibility of having children. Could she possibly be lucky enough to have both?

"I am not overemotional," Nelly snapped and gave him a defiant look. "Frantor saved my life and I've never had a chance to thank him before."

"He knows how grateful we are." Artek's arms tightened around Nelly as he dipped his head to Frantor.

Before Frantor could respond, a big pink-furred male came bounding over, dragging a pretty dark-haired girl who Florie recognized as Pearl's sister Ruby.

"You're the cook, aren't you? Did you bring any food?"

Ruby rolled her eyes, and smiled at Florie. "I'm sorry, but all he thinks about is his stomach."

"Not just my stomach." he purred into the girl's ear. "I chose you, didn't I, even though you can't cook."

Florie was still too stunned to respond, but Frantor shook his head.

"Actually, we came to join you for dinner, if that's all right with you, Nelly?"

"We have plenty," Nelly assured him. "That is if we can stop Benjar from eating it all."

The pink male assumed a look of exaggerated innocence, and Nelly laughed, her tears vanishing.

"And speaking of dinner, it's ready. I'll just grab a couple of extra plates."

Everyone began to follow Nelly out of the room, but each of the males stopped long enough to greet Frantor and to introduce their brides. Of course his brothers had seen his scars before, but she was grateful that none of the women showed any dismay. Somehow she managed to smile and respond appropriately, even though her mind was still whirling.

"Is something wrong, sweetheart?" Frantor asked as soon as they were alone.

"Nelly is pregnant?"

"Yes, she is."

"We—I mean we humans—can have your babies, even though we are different species?"

"That's what Artek said." He put his arms around her, frowning down at her. "If you are concerned about earlier, then do not be. All of us have a birth control implant to prevent our seed from becoming fertile."

Her heart sank.

"Is that because you don't want children?"

He hesitated. "When we first came here, all we wanted was space to heal. But now I think it's more. We're building a legacy, and children are part of that."

"Can the implant be reversed?"

"Yes. It's a simple matter to remove, and the reversal is effective immediately."

She clutched his hand, her heart pounding. "I know everything has happened really quickly, and we haven't even talked about it, but I would really like a child—a child with you. You don't have to tell me right now if you need to think about it," she added quickly.

"Think about having a baby with you?" His smile was wide and happy, despite the scar twisting one corner. "I can't think of anything I'd like better."

"Really? Then let's get it done tonight."

His smile suddenly faltered and she gave him an anxious look.

"What's wrong? Are you having second thoughts? Do you need more time?"

"No, that's not it. But what... what if the baby is scared of me because of how I look?"

Her heart melted as she put her arms around him.

"Our baby will never be scared of you. Our baby will grow up loving you just the way you are, just the way I do."

He shuddered, and then his body relaxed.

"I'll ask Drakkar to remove the implant tonight."

Happiness filled her so completely she felt as if she were glowing. Only a short time ago she'd been convinced she would live out her life alone, but now she had Frantor and, with any luck at all, a baby as well. Everything was perfect.

EPILOGUE

Nine months later...

"How's the new prosthetic working out?" Drakkar asked as Frantor escorted him to the outside door.

"It's fine," he said impatiently. "What about Florie and the baby?"

Florie and Drakkar had finally convinced him to have his prosthetic replaced. The trip to the medical center in Port Cantor had been as terrible as he had anticipated, bringing back far too many memories of his previous trips. Only the presence of his pregnant mate had stopped him from turning around and retreating to the ranch. He had woken from the surgery with familiar spikes of agony radiating from his shoulder, and he'd been quite sure that the procedure had been a waste of time. But the pain faded surprisingly quickly, and within a very short time he was using his arm as easily as if it were his natural arm.

He hadn't realized until after he was no longer experiencing it how much the constant pain from his previous prosthetic had worn on him.

The rest of his body was better as well. The scars would never fade, but Drakkar and Florie had developed a regimen of massage and stretching which helped to relieve a lot of his previous pain. And of course, it didn't hurt that he slept soundly every night after making love to his beautiful wife.

"You would tell me if there was an issue, wouldn't you?" Drakkar asked again.

"Probably not," he said honestly, "but Florie would make me. Honestly, it feels fine. What about Florie and the baby?"

"Their scans were perfect. Now I'm going to leave you alone with your wife and your child and return to my own family." Drakkar hesitated, and clasped his uninjured shoulder. "I am very happy for you, my brother."

"And I am very grateful to you. If you hadn't saved my life, I would never have been lucky enough to have this."

Drakkar's hand tightened briefly on his shoulder, and then he was gone in a flutter of wings. Frantor returned to the upper floor of the mill, smiling as he always did at the changes that had taken place. The small kitchen table had been replaced by a much larger one—a necessity given how often people showed up at dinner time to eat Florie's cooking. They had also acquired a comfortable couch as well as another large chair.

The bedroom area had been partitioned off, and he paused at the entrance to admire his bride. Florie was propped up against the pillows, looking more beautiful than ever as she smiled down at their son as he nursed eagerly at her breast. He bent down to kiss her, curving his hand over her other breast and tugging gently at the engorged nipple, smiling at the resulting pearl of liquid. The changes her body had undergone during her pregnancy fascinated him—fascinated and aroused him.

She shook her head at him, but her eyes were smiling.

"Drakkar said no fooling around until after my next checkup."

"Does this count as fooling around?" he asked, tugging a little harder on her nipple and hearing her breath catch. She had enjoyed his explorations almost as much as he had.

"Why don't we discuss it later? After our son is asleep." She gave him a rueful smile. "Assuming that he does sleep. Nelly told me not to expect to get a lot of rest."

He immediately started to withdraw his hand, feeling guilty, but she caught it and pressed it back against the lush mound.

"Some things are worth losing sleep over. But I think Ermek is already falling asleep."

They had named the baby after his father, and in an odd way he felt as if the baby reconnected him with the family he had lost.

She gently detached the baby from her breast, then handed him over. He gathered the small body close, but his heart was pounding. In spite of Florie's acceptance, and the acceptance of everyone in the valley, he couldn't help remembering those long-ago fears of terrified children running from him. At least Ermek was asleep.

But when he looked down, the baby's eyes were wide open. He had his mother's eyes, huge and green, and they stared up at him as he held his breath. Drakkar had told him that it might take a little while for the baby to learn how to focus, but he could have sworn that Ermek was studying his face. He returned the solemn green stare, and then the baby's lips pursed in what he was convinced was a smile. He breezed a shuddering sigh of relief even as Ermek's eyes closed again.

"He smiled at me," he whispered.

"I'm sure he did. I'm sure he knows he has a father who will always love him and protect him," she said solemnly, and then she smiled. "Now go put him in his crib and let's have some cuddle time while we can."

"Naked cuddle time?"

He still felt the same thrill every time their skin touched.

"Of course naked cuddle time."

"I'll be right back."

He grinned as he placed the baby in the crib, then stripped off his clothes and went to join her. As he pulled her into his arms, her hand skated over the scars on his side, but he no longer felt broken. Thanks to Florie, he was whole once more.

AUTHOR'S NOTE

Thank you so much for reading **Frantor**! I've been dying to write his story ever since he showed up in Artek. He tugged at my heartstrings just as he did at Florie's, but I'm so glad he found his happy ending. I hope you are as well!

Whether you enjoyed the story or not, it would mean the world to me if you left an honest review on Amazon – reviews are one of the best ways to help other readers find my books!

As usual, I have to thank my readers for coming on these adventures with me - I couldn't do it without you!

And, as always, a special thanks to my beta team – Janet S, Nancy V, and Kitty S. Your thoughts and comments are incredibly helpful!

Up next!

AUTHOR'S NOTE

Seven Brides for Seven Alien Brothers continues with ***Gilmat!***

Can love bloom between a bookish human and a giant alien? And when outside forces threaten the ranch, can Gilmat call on his heritage in order to save Julie - and the rest of his family?

Gilmat is available on Amazon!

To make sure you don't miss out on any new releases, please visit my website and sign up for my newsletter!

www.honeyphillips.com

OTHER TITLES

Seven Brides for Seven Alien Brothers

Artek

Benjar

Callum

Drakkar

Endark

Frantor

Gilmat

The Alien Abduction Series

Anna and the Alien

Beth and the Barbarian

Cam and the Conqueror

Deb and the Demon

Ella and the Emperor

Faith and the Fighter

Greta and the Gargoyle

Hanna and the Hitman

Izzie and the Icebeast

Joan and the Juggernaut

Kate and the Kraken

Lily and the Lion

Mary and the Minotaur

Nancy and the Naga

Olivia and the Orc

Pandora and the Prisoner

Quinn and the Queller

The Alien Invasion Series

Alien Selection

Alien Conquest

Alien Prisoner

Alien Breeder

Alien Alliance

Alien Hope

Exposed to the Elements

The Naked Alien

The Bare Essentials

A Nude Attitude

The Buff Beast

The Strip Down

Folsom Planet Blues

Alien Most Wanted: Caged Beast

Alien Most Wanted: Prison Mate

Alien Most Wanted: Mastermind

Alien Most Wanted: Unchained

Monster Between the Sheets

Extra Virgin Gargoyle

Without a Stitch

Sweet Monster Treats

Cupcakes for My Orc Enemy

Cyborgs on Mars

High Plains Cyborg

The Good, the Bad, and the Cyborg

A Fistful of Cyborg

A Few Cyborgs More

The Magnificent Cyborg

The Outlaw Cyborg

The Cyborg with No Name

Treasured by the Alien

Mama and the Alien Warrior

A Son for the Alien Warrior

Daughter of the Alien Warrior

A Family for the Alien Warrior

The Nanny and the Alien Warrior

A Home for the Alien Warrior

A Gift for the Alien Warrior

A Treasure for the Alien Warrior

Cosmic Fairy Tales

Jackie and the Giant

Horned Holidays

Krampus and the Crone

A Gift for Nicholas

A Kiss of Frost

Blind Date with an Alien

Her Alien Farmhand

Stranded with an Alien

A SciFi Holiday Tail

Sinta

ABOUT THE AUTHOR

USA Today bestselling author Honey Phillips writes steamy science fiction stories about hot alien warriors and the human women they can't resist. From abductions to invasions, the ride might be rough, but the end always satisfies.

Honey wrote and illustrated her first book at the tender age of five. Her writing has improved since then. Her drawing skills, unfortunately, have not. She loves writing, reading, traveling, cooking, and drinking champagne - not necessarily in that order.

Honey loves to hear from her wonderful readers! You can stalk her at any of the following locations...

www.facebook.com/HoneyPhillipsAuthor
www.bookbub.com/authors/honey-phillips
www.instagram.com/HoneyPhillipsAuthor
www.honeyphillips.com

Printed in Great Britain
by Amazon